AN ILLUSTRATED
AUTOBIOGRAPHY

Santa

MY LIFE & TIMES

CREATOR BIOS

Bill Sienkiewicz has had a major impact on the field of comic books and graphic novels with his innovative use of collage, illustration, and storytelling techniques. He has been honored with many major awards in the United States and abroad, including the prestigious Yellow Kid award, and has exhibited his art worldwide. He received an Emmy nomination for his work on the animated television series *"Where in the World is Carmen Sandiego?"*

Santa Claus, known primarily for his unparalleled work on Christmas Eve delivering toys to every child in the world, is a gifted carpenter and toymaker and keen environmentalist. This autobiography, written in conjunction with Jared Green, is Santa's first book, although he is currently considering a series of books about a part-time private investigator and toy maker who solves mysteries around the world.

Jared Green is an associate professor of English literature at Stonehill College. In addition to scholarly work on literature, anthropology, visual culture, and cinema, he has published poetry and edited books on hip-hop and electronic music. His fiction has been recognized by the Martha's Vineyard Institute for Creative Writing with a MVICW Fellowship, and by the state of Rhode Island with a Robert and Margaret MaColl Johnson Fellowship. *Santa Claus: The Illustrated Autobiography* marks his first collaboration with Santa.

Martin I. Green is the Director of Berkshire Studio Productions and the creator, producer, and co-author of several bestselling books, including the Jimi Hendrix biography, *Voodoo Child*, as well as *A Sigh of Relief: The First-aid Handbook for Childhood Emergencies, Lifesavers,* and *Been Here and Gone: A Memoir of the Blues* (with David Dalton).

AN ILLUSTRATED
AUTOBIOGRAPHY

Santa

MY LIFE & TIMES

AS TOLD TO
Jared Green

ILLUSTRATED BY
Bill Sienkiewicz

TITAN
COMICS

SANTA: MY LIFE & TIMES. AN ILLUSTRATED AUTOBIOGRAPHY

ISBN: 9781787732223

Published by Titan Comics, a registered trademark of Titan Publishing Group Ltd., 144 Southwark St., London SE1 0UP.

A CIP catalogue record for this title is available from the British Library.

First Edition October 2019

1 3 5 7 9 10 8 6 4 2

Printed in China

What did you think of this book? We love to hear from our readers. Please email us at: readerfeedback@titanemail.com, or write to us at the above address. To receive advance information, news competitions, and exclusive offers online, please sign up for the Titan newsletter on our website: titan-comics.com

Created, designed and produced by MARTIN I. GREEN
As Told to JARED F. GREEN
Illustrated by BILL SIENKIEWICZ
Creative Consultant WILL EISNER

With much appreciation to Lou Aronica for his extraordinary enthusiasm, support and unwavering belief.

And a very special thank you to Marc Jaffe; Roger Cooper; Ian Ballantine and Bill Shinker
for their years of ongoing encouragement and support.

Thanks also to the following for their invaluable help during the various phases of this project:
Leo K. Barnes; Marcia and Saul "Bo" Bolotsky; Bessie Boris; Sam Davol; Martha Donovan;
Alan Douglas; Gail Firestone; Leo Garel; Peggy Gordon; Henry and Helen Green; Gloria Henry;
Adria S. Hillman; J.A.C. Lithographers (color separations & film); Rosie Keefe; George Pratt;
Arthur and Adele Puhn; Kim Ragone; Seymour V. Reit; Harvey Rottenberg; Richard P. Rubinstein;
Steven V. Rubin; Ben Schawinsky; Jessie G. Schoonmaker; Laura and Alvin Sinderbrand;
Anne Sipp; Lynne West and Joe Zucker.

For all children everywhere,
each of you a brilliant star,
all of you the world's bright dream.
With much love,
SANTA

For my parents, who taught me to believe.
For Mary, who never stopped believing.
For Jared, who made me believe again.
And
for Anne Sipp, whose kindness, generosity and love
are equalled only by Santa's.
MIG

A Cup of Tea

*I*t was all upon a quiet Christmas morning, as chilly a day as any I can remember, when I was invited in for a cup of tea. Dawn was just breaking as I approached a familiar wooden house with its blue tin roof; a house that had once marked the end of my Yuletide journeys. I hadn't visited this little place in many years, but now I felt drawn to it, and I soon discovered why: it was once again aglow with the brightness of childhood. Inside, I found two new stockings hung by the fireplace, emptied of all but the wishes of two little children awaiting the delights of their very first Christmas.

As I filled the new stockings with toys and sweets, I thought of the first time I had visited this house and of the little girl whose greatest wish had been to one day ride with the reindeer. I remembered, too, how she had always tried to catch me leaving the presents, even when she had grown up and had children of her own. She had never seemed to lose her childlike spirit, and now she had her great-grandchildren to share it with. How quickly the time passes.

Smiling to myself, I lit up the colored lights on the tree and was just about to rise back up the chimney when I heard a soft sound from the room behind me. As I turned, my gaze met with the marvelous grin of a small and aged woman whom I knew in an instant was none other than that very same little girl, come to catch me in the act at last.

"One hundred years have I waited for this chance," she said in a voice that was barely a whisper. "Now won't you join me for a cup of tea?"

So we sat together by the fireside, two old friends talking of our memories of each other and of all that had happened since her childhood days. She showed me the toys she had saved from Christmases long past, and as we sipped our tea, she asked me all the questions that children have been asking since I first began my visits. Where did I come from? Are there such things as elves? How do the reindeer fly, and how does a belly as big as mine fit down all those little chimneys?

Then, when I had answered all of them from first to last, she looked at me with a smile and said: "Do you remember my wish?" And of course I did.

High above the rooftops of her village we flew, the reindeer soaring over snow-tipped forests and ice-covered lakes while my old friend shrieked with delight. Up, up past the wintry clouds we rose, and there we stayed until the bright morning sun came to waken the children from their Christmas dreams.

When at last it was time to leave, she bade me goodbye with a kiss on the cheek, and I could see even as I sped away how her eyes shone like those of a young girl. She had told me that she always remembered that little girl inside of her and could still see me as plain as day, long after her friends had forgotten how.

As I rode home that Christmas morning, I kept thinking of the words she had whispered to me as we parted: "Yours is a story that wants telling." she had said. And she was right, for I have always wished that I could take the time to sit; with each and every child, answering the questions that have gone too long unanswered. Now is the time to do just that.

This book you now hold in your hands is a wish that came true not so very long ago, with a cup of Christmas tea and the innocent wonder of a most unusual one-hundred-year-old little girl. It is for her, and for you, and for all the children everywhere who know to believe in magic that the tales in this book have been written.

And I promise you that every word is true.

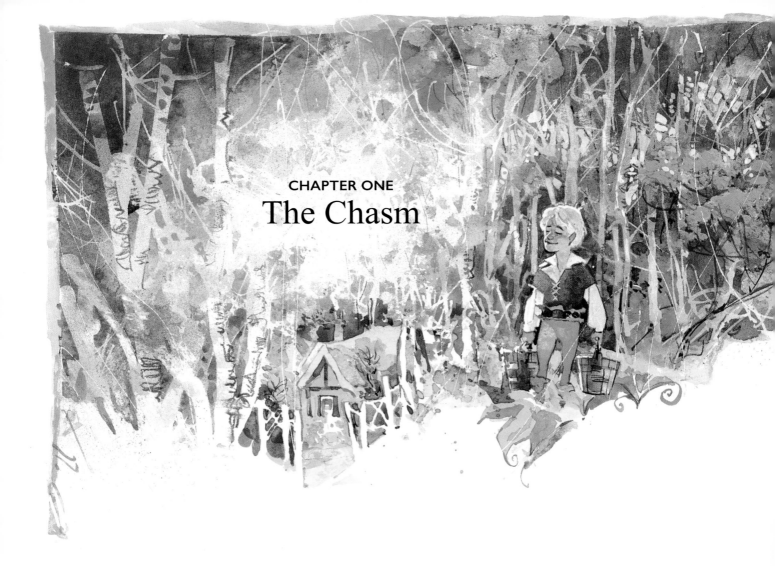

CHAPTER ONE
The Chasm

*A*s children, we all have secret places to ourselves; those places where it seems that no one else has ever been, where we can go to imagine the world however we wish. Old though I am, I still have such a place. It lies just at the edge of the vast northern pine forest where I have lived since my boyhood days. Even then, I was aware of the special friendship that I share with the forest. There, among the ageless trees and wild woodland creatures, I grew to feel more at peace than anywhere else, as if somehow I knew it was where I belonged. Many is the morning I have spent at my secret place, daydreaming while the mists weave their way through the quiet wood. At these times, I can see myself as a young boy once again, wandering through the same misty region that has gone unchanged since that morning so long ago, when my life's tale truly began.

In those days long past, I lived in a small cottage with my father, Anselm, and my mother, Gerda, leading the simple and carefree life of a young 15-year boy. It was in the hours before breakfast on one particular day that I set out, a bucket in either hand, to fetch water from the falls just beyond our doorstep.

With the light summer breeze at my back, I began to sing the woods-walking song I had made up for days just like this one:

Shortest by near
And longest by far,
Timtwiddle, tumtwiddle,
Sun, moon, and star.

Tall things and short things,
Red apples are blue,
Right foot and left foot,
Both in one shoe.

Trees in the sky
And clouds on the ground,
A circle's a square
That knows its way 'round.

Longest by near
And shortest by far,
Tumtwiddle, timtwiddle,
Sun, moon, and star.

There was not a thing about that morning that so much as whispered of the wondrous events that were soon to unfold. Still, as life will have its whim, the most astonishing things often seem to spring from the most ordinary beginnings.

Since the walk to the falls was one I had taken many times before, you can imagine how strange it was that this time the usual sound of rushing water was not to be heard. I stopped in my tracks for a moment and strained my ears to listen:

Shhheeee, huhrusssshhh, shhhheeerussshhhhh, said the wind in the pines. But the water said nothing.

Tsssskk, trsssskkk, trrruusssskkkk, said the leaves beneath my feet. But the water said nothing.

Criiick, chuck chuck, Crrriiiiick, chuck chuck, said the squirrels in the boughs, and *Rumblumbdunderummmbumbumbernuk!* said the nuts rolled by the squirrels.

And still the water said nothing. In fact, no sooner had I reached the clearing where the falls should have been than I realized that there was no water at all. That was when I noticed the first of what were to be many peculiar things that morning.

What I discovered in place of the falls was, as you will see, only somewhat peculiar compared to what was in store. Nonetheless, I was amazed to find that a smooth tunnel had been carved into the stony face of the hill where the water usually ran. Of course curiosity got the better of me, and I drew nearer to inspect the passage. Finding it to be just large enough for me to squeeze through, that's what I did.

At the far end of the tunnel I came upon a path winding through a stretch of forest the likes of which I had never seen before. Here, a silence more ancient than the land itself seemed to hang in the still air. The trees had the gnarled look of skeletons, and their branches bent to the ground as though a tremendous weight had settled upon them. The farther I walked, the stranger that forest became. Beneath my feet, the soft green carpet of moss gave way to stones and cruel brambles that tore my clothing as I passed. A thin layer of yellow dust blanketed everything in sight with a pale hue like the surface of the moon. No breeze stirred the boughs, and no birds dared to sing.

I soon grew uneasy, having wandered far out of my way into that unfamiliar territory, but when I turned to retrace my steps, I saw that the path had vanished behind me, along with the tunnel and the hills. For miles in every direction, there was only the strange and forbidding forest. My one choice was to keep following the path still ahead of me in the hope of arriving someplace friendly.

But then, both the path and my hopes along with it came to an abrupt end, as I found myself at the edge of a gaping chasm with nowhere to turn. There was no doubt about it; I was hopelessly lost, and not a soul would know where to find me.

Then, suddenly, a melancholy sound broke through the stillness. So soft and low was the noise that at first I thought it might have been my own, but then I heard it again: a gentle cry like

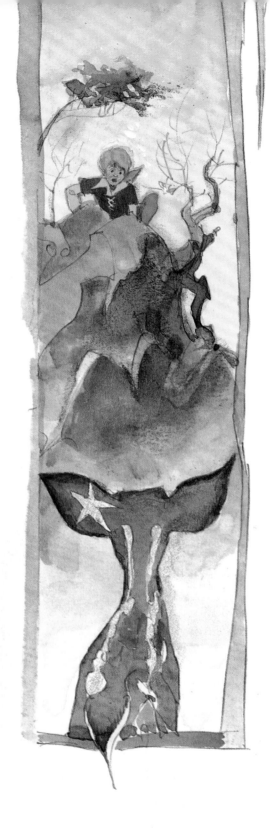

the whine of a rusty wheel. Cautiously, I peered over the edge of the chasm. There, staring back at me, were the frightened eyes of a little fawn.

Trapped on a narrow ledge between me and the depthless gorge, he gazed up at me expectantly, as if knowing that I was his only hope. I looked toward the gloomy trees, searching for vines or something that might prove useful, but to no avail; these woods were not about to offer me their services. I would just have to climb down myself.

"Well, little one," I said, trying to reassure him, "it looks like you'll have to trust me. I'll get us out of here whether this forest likes it or not."

Drawing a deep breath, I lowered myself over the edge and began the treacherous descent. Not daring to look down, I let my feet search blindly for support as the aged stone turned to sand beneath my fingers. Somehow I managed to hold on as I continued the climb down. And then I finally felt the ledge under my feet.

Not knowing what my next step would be, I sat down, appreciating that little ledge more than all the comforts of the world. The fawn edged closer to me and nudged my hand. He was a beautiful creature, small but strong, with a gentle face and a magnificent marking, shaped just like the morning star, illuminating his left ear. He seemed to understand that, for the moment, the chasm had made companions of us.

"Hello, friend," I said as I stroked his neck, "I don't suppose you might have any suggestions to help us out now, do you?"

I know you might think that it was silly of me to ask such a question, but if there's one thing I've learned that I think you should remember, it's to always listen to what the animals have to tell us. So then, when the fawn gave my shirt a gentle tug, I knew just what I had to do.

Spreading the shirt on the ground, I coaxed the fawn into the center and fashioned a kind of carrying pouch. With my passenger securely on my back, my hands were free for the upward climb. This time, the cliffside seemed even steeper than before, and the crumbling rocks threatened to send us back down into the yawning chasm. Yet on we went, inch by inch and hand over hand, until eventually we reached the top. At last, I pulled myself over the edge and loosened the bundle, setting the fawn free.

That's when the considerably peculiar thing happened. Looking back at me over his shoulder, the fawn actually seemed to smile.

Then turning toward the woods, he bounded three times and, with a twitch of his tail, flew up into the sky.

So astonished was I that I stumbled backwards, teetering dangerously near the edge of the chasm. Before I could regain my balance, the rocks crumbled beneath me, and over I went.

It all happened so quickly that I remember very little of the fall itself, save for the faint smell of sweet poppies and the cloud of blue butterflies that rose from the depths in a fluttering squall. Behind them, there came the chasm floor, rushing to meet me with its long stalagmite fingers. I hardly had time to shut my eyes before I felt the awful shock that I knew would be my finish. But it wasn't — and this is the most peculiar thing of all, for there I was, neither dead nor dreaming, but suspended upside down by an unseen force, my head just inches from the ground.

All around me was a magnificent sea of colored poppies, and lovely music filled my unbelieving ears. And there, too, right before my eyes where one would least expect to find them, were a pair of three-toed feet wiggling a smart salute.

"Greetings, young Nicholas. You have arrived just in time."

CHAPTER TWO

The Oracle

When at last I was set right side up, my bewildered eyes beheld those of the strangest old man I had ever seen. He was no bigger than half my size, and despite his long and pointed nose, his features were gentle, as though they had been carved out of soft wood. Long white hair flowed from beneath the peak of his cap, twining down his shoulders where it met with the hairs of his beard. He was clothed entirely in a moss-colored robe that hung right down to his unusual feet. In one hand, he held a set of wooden pipes while with the other, he gestured as he spoke.

"Oh yes, Nicholas. We have known all about you for quite some time. I beg your pardon for the necessity of your fall, yes, but there was simply no other way. I assure you there is nothing to fear from us, no."

I wanted desperately to say something, to ask him who he was or why he had tricked me so cruelly, yet suddenly I found myself unable to speak a word. The little man put a finger to his nose and chuckled.

"I am afraid you will find that your words make no sound down here, Nicholas. But that is not to be your concern, no. For now you must only listen, and listen well. There is nothing that happens by accident, Nicholas; everything has a reason. The time has come for you to begin your work, yes. Your misstep has taken you to the very threshold of your destiny, indeed it has. Now you must seek your rightful path, and in seeking, find. Ah, you wonder 'why', yes? That I cannot answer for you. There are some questions that best answer themselves."

Beneath his overhanging eyebrows, a sly glimmer lit his eyes. Raising the pipes to his lips, he began to play a soft melody, and the air was filled with music:

> *Need and greed*
> *Hold many in thrall,*
> *Yet who, despite riches,*
> *Is the poorest of all?*

As he continued to play, he melted slowly into the shadows of the flowers, until only the last strains of his song remained:

> *Deep in seeds of giving lie*
> *Fruit and flower of living.*
> *The fortunate need not ask why,*
> *It is all a matter of knowing....*

When the last echoes of the piping faded, the chasm grew cold and I found myself alone again; tired, hungry, and terribly confused by all that had just happened. Who was that strange little man, and what could he have meant when he spoke of my rightful path? More importantly, how on earth would I find any path if I couldn't even find my way out of the chasm?

Just then, a blinding light burst forth, and, as if led in silent symphony by an unseen hand, the poppies began to unfold their petals, revealing tiny shimmering creatures within. Soon the gorge was alive with the whispering sound of wings in flight and the splendor of countless woodsprites, each more beautiful than the flower that bore it. They circled around me, soft and melodious like luminous hummingbirds, beckoning for me to follow.

The sea of poppies swayed to one side, revealing a small stone archway in the cliff. Through this narrow passage I crawled, the dazzling sprites lighting the way up into the very heart of the chasm wall.

As the climb grew steeper, the tunnel began to change: what began as bare stone soon turned into opals and deep red rubies, turning then to silver and smooth polished gold. The passage widened and opened out into a great crystal hall, where the looking-glass walls reflected my face without end. Beyond its far doorway, we came upon a valley of broad toadstools, loud with the hum of sapphire and emerald dragonflies.

In the center of the valley, I found a pool of sweet water and drank deeply, hardly breathing between sips. As a strange tingling sensation came over me, the last thought to cross my mind was that I could not see my reflection on the surface of the water.

The next thing I knew, I awoke to feel the spray of the waterfall gently tickling my face. As though they had been no more than dreams, the desolate woods, the enchanted chasm, and the woodsprites all had vanished. Here, there was only clear water racing down the stream through the swaying pines. And though I searched up and down the stony hillside, the mysterious passageway was nowhere to be found.

CHAPTER THREE
Anselm and Gerda

t length I returned home to bed and fell into a deep, deep sleep and slept motionless until the following afternoon. In that time, I dreamt of strange fabulous beasts and gossamer birds that danced about me in wild circles; I dreamt of blossoms falling like rain on the streets of the village; again and again, I saw myself falling to the depths of the chasm, and inside the poppies were a thousand laughing children. Throughout these haunting images I could hear the little man's words echoing:

> *Deep in seeds of giving lie*
> *Fruit and flower of living.*
> *The fortunate need not ask why,*
> *It is all a matter of knowing....*

When I awoke, I found my father seated at the edge of my bed with a bowl of stew and fresh bread.

I took the meal and, eating feverishly, told him between mouthfuls all that had happened. Anselm, my father, listened patiently, nodding only slightly at all the fantastic details of my story. When I had finished, he looked at me with a knowing smile. My mother, Gerda, who had been standing in the doorway all the while, came forward and clasped his hand. He looked up at her, still nodding, and said:

"No, my boy, I'm not surprised. I knew from the moment I found you that you were somehow surrounded by magic. Now the time has come for you to know the whole story, Nicholas..."

I'd always known that Anselm and Gerda were not my natural parents, for ever since I had been a young child they had always made certain that I understood how I had come into the family.

Before I arrived, they had already shared many happy years of marriage, content in all ways but one; they had yet to be blessed with the child they had longed for. Then one morning, while gathering wood in the forest, Anselm had stumbled upon me, a tiny baby sheltered beneath the boughs of a holly tree. There was not another soul in sight, and, unable to find the slightest clue as to how I had gotten there, Anselm took me home to Gerda, where they cared for me as though I were their own.

That was the story as I knew it, but as I learned that afternoon after my adventure, there was still more to be told. What I didn't know was that Anselm had been led into the desolate woods by a

vision of a tremendous white stag that had appeared to him at dawn. There, at the edge of the very same chasm I had just described, he discovered me nestled in thistledown, upon a bed of poppy petals.

It was then that he knew his dream had come true; his family was at last complete.

"Never have I been so happy as that magical day, Nicholas," continued Anselm. "But the strangest part is that no matter how I tried, I could never find my way back to the chasm again. It was as if the forest had opened just for that one morning and just so I could find you. Perhaps those woods only reveal themselves for very special reasons."

"But why for me?" I asked, anxious to solve the mystery. "And what about all the other things I saw? What about the old man and his riddles? What can they mean?"

"Well, it just may be that the old legends are true after all," he answered, taking me by the hand. "Come with me, Nicholas, I have something to show you."

He brought me into his workshop, where the last glow of daylight illumined the tools and papers and wooden figurines that cluttered the shelves. From behind the rows of dusty bottles and broken clocks, he produced a small book bound in smooth treebark. The faded gold lettering on the cover read: *The Book of the Hills, Being a Guide to the Little People.*

"My great-grandfather made this book ages ago, Nicholas, in the time when it's said that humans shared this land with all sorts of fairy folk. He recorded tales of every one of them on these pages; perhaps he even knew of your mysterious little man."

And sure enough, among the many accounts written in my ancestor's spidery script, we found the legend of the elves and the lost kingdom of Elfhame. I had heard tales of such creatures before, at the summer storytelling festivals, but I had always thought they had been made up for our amusement. Now, however, I began to realize that it was not so, for the book's air of solemn truth left little room for any doubt.

It said that the elves were a race of crafty artisans, rumored to have magical powers and fabulous wealth. And ruling over all of the elfin tribes was the most powerful of them all, the mysterious piper known as Elder, who made his dwelling in a mystical gorge deep within the northernmost woodland.

No more was written about him, but even that was enough to assure me that this Elder fellow and the old man of the chasm were one and the same.

Knowing his name proved to be little help, though, for now I was just as confused as ever. If he was truly as powerful as the book had said, then what could he possibly want with me, the adopted son of a simple carpenter unlearned in the ways of the world? And what could the Elder have had in mind when he spoke those puzzling rhymes?

While I sat lost in thought, my father had returned to his workbench and was busy putting the finishing touches on a cradle he had made for a neighbor's newborn infant. I watched him then just as I had when I was a little boy, amazed at how he could bring forth unseen riches from an ordinary piece of wood. With his talents for carving, he could surely have been a masterful sculptor or a fine toymaker, but he had chosen instead to devote his skills to helping our friends and neighbors. He was always out fixing roofs or repairing barns or building furniture for people in the nearby towns. He rarely accepted money for his efforts, preferring instead to exchange his labor for whatever a family was able to give, be it food, supplies, or services of their own.

I remember how he always used to tell me that of all his greatest joys, he had loved nothing more than teaching me the secrets of his craft. As a young boy, I would always use broken branches and fashion wooden sabres for pirate games, or make crude puppets and put on shows for all my friends. Even then, my parents encouraged my hobby, and they both used to say that the true secret to happiness is to find something you love and spend your life doing it.

Well, I loved to make things with my hands, and in all the world, there was nothing I wanted to be more than a carpenter like my father. And so, while my friends were off dreaming of conquering the high seas and exploring the darkest jungles, I stayed at my father's side and slowly learned the woodworker's craft. But this was really all that I knew, and now I somehow had to fulfill a prophecy

that I didn't even understand. Within one single day, my own future seemed to have grown as vast and mysterious as the forest itself.

My father interrupted my reverie, gesturing for me to join him. As I hammered the last pegs into the cradle's headboard, he turned to me and said:

"Do you know why I like giving gifts, Nicholas? I'll tell you. It's because it keeps me from feeling poor. Why, even the simplest things become priceless when they are given out of love. That's why you can never feel poor if you're able to give something to someone."

From the back of my mind, I heard again the whispers of Elder's riddle.

Need and greed
Hold many in thrall,
Yet who, despite riches,
Is the poorest of all?

Suddenly, it seemed so very simple. Anselm himself had spoken the answer: the truly needy are those who cannot share their wealth or possessions. Still, that answer solved only one part of the puzzle. Much to my disappointment, I found the mystery of the oracle to be elusive as ever, and it was not until several months later that another encounter in the forest would show me the way.

CHAPTER FOUR

The Old Woodsman and the Magic Door

It was January of the new year, and a strange winter wind had caused one of our neighbor's children, a young boy named Jaspar, to fall gravely ill. One afternoon, after my mother had visited the child with her remedies of hot broth and lemon balm tonic, the sadness in her eyes told me that something was troubling her. When I asked her about it, she replied:

"Oh, Nicholas, I'm very worried about that little boy. His family can't afford doctors to care for him, and he doesn't have any playthings to help take his mind off his illness. What if you gave him one of your old toys? I'm sure it would make him feel much better if he had something to play with. Why don't you bring him that music box that you loved when you were young?"

Now you must understand that, though I didn't wish to appear selfish in front of my mother (and especially not with Elder's words still echoing in my mind), the mere thought of parting with such a treasure seemed unthinkable. Father and I had made the music box when I was just a boy. It was my favorite toy, and it was still the one possession that I prized most, for I had never seen its equal. It was shaped like a miniature carousel, with painted camels and elephants and eight tiny wooden horses that I had carved myself and which, at the turn of a key, would spin and dance to my favorite melody. There was simply no way I could ever part with it.

Sensing my reluctance, Mother suggested that perhaps I might let him play with it for just a little while. I agreed and promptly set out for Jaspar's home with the music box tucked beneath my coat. His mother greeted me so warmly when I arrived that I felt a little ashamed for not really wanting to be there. She led me straight to her son's room where he lay beneath a threadbare blanket, his face wet with tears and his dark eyes glittering with fever. I unwrapped the music box and, placing it in his hands, turned the key.

The music began, and the horses all danced, rising and falling in giddy circles. Jaspar stopped crying and turned his attention to the fabulous toy. He watched with widening eyes as the mirrors on the carousel sent patterns of sunlight spinning about the room. Slowly, a smile spread across his face, and he began to giggle so much that I couldn't help laughing too. Soon, the two of us were making so much gleeful noise that we could barely hear the music.

On and on the horses danced until the little boy had giggled himself into a deep, peaceful sleep. I gently removed the music box from his hands and wrapped it up, ready to return home. At the door his mother whispered gratefully:

"Thank you so much, Nicholas. You've made him laugh for the first time in weeks. What a truly wonderful toy you have. You must feel very proud."

But I wasn't very proud at all. In fact, on my way home I began to feel more than a little bit guilty for having taken the music box back with me. I thought of how delighted Jaspar had been and how good it had felt to have helped ease his illness. But then he was only a little child, I reasoned, and surely he wouldn't be able to appreciate it as much as I did. And what if he broke it? Then it would be lost and I could never replace it. Maybe I would find him another music box, and he wouldn't have to know the difference. Determined to stick to my resolution, I clutched my bundle and continued on my way.

Suddenly, I became aware that gales of loud laughter were drifting through the snowcapped trees. Curious as to who else might be out on such a cold day, I followed the sound and found its source to be an old woodsman, sitting on a stool in the midst of a wide clearing. I watched him for a bit and saw that, every now and then, he would let out a whooping burst of laughter and roll on the ground, waving his arms about wildly. I decided to approach him and ask him to share the joke.

"Well, my boy, I am laughing because nothing could be more wonderful than watching the stars on a night like this," came the reply, followed by another thundering whoop that blew his long wispy beard over the top of his head.

"But sir," I said politely, hoping not to offend him, "there are no stars. It's still daytime."

"Aha!" he said, standing on his stool like a statue. "It is daytime for you because you can only see the sun. As for me, I am blind, and so I choose to see the stars." And with that, he whooped again and came crashing to the ground. I ran to pick him up, and, feeling terribly embarrassed for not having noticed that he was blind, I mumbled a hasty apology.

"Nonsense, nonsense!" he replied, tying his beard into a knot to keep it in place. "I wasn't always blind, you know. But my life has been long and I've seen a good many things, so I gave my sight to an earthworm who wished to watch the sunrise. Now I'm free to look at whatever my heart desires. But oh my! Why are you standing out in the cold like that? Come in, my boy, come in!" Puzzled at the odd suggestion, I asked:

"Pardon me, sir, but inside where?"

"Inside where?" he said, tweaking my nose smartly. "Why, inside my house, of course!"

Now I suppose that after my adventure at the chasm, I should have been used to peculiar goings-on, but this fellow seemed terribly mixed up, so I thought it only reasonable to point out that we were both outside in the forest, with no house in sight.

"Bosh!" the old woodsman shouted, as he balanced himself on his finger. "It's all in how you look at it, my boy. You don't see any house because I gave all of my wood and stones to a village in need of a new schoolroom. Yet still I'm kept warm and dry, and now I have more room than I know what to do with. Look around and see for yourself!"

"I see," I replied, not seeing anything at all. Clearly, I was in over my head, and so, hoping not to excite him any further, I inched toward the edge of the clearing and called out:

"Well, it's been nice meeting you, sir, but if you'll excuse me, I must be on my way." "Your way!" bellowed the woodsman.

"How perfectly impolite! Who's to say it's your way when it could just as easily be mine? But then, you seem to be in need of one of your own, so I'll let you have it."

"Now see here..." I began, getting quite frustrated.

"Well, which is it?" he interrupted from beneath his stool. "See or hear? They're quite different, you know, and you shouldn't mix them up like that or you won't know a sneeze from a snail.

You're an awfully confusing boy, you know. But if you must go all the same, be sure to pick a bouquet of flowers before you do." I knew it was just asking for trouble, but I thought I should make it clear to the old man that he didn't have any flowers to pick.

"Ah!" he replied, putting both feet behind his ears. "That's because I gave them all to a young girl who had never before smelled a rose. Now my garden is bigger and more beautiful than ever. Don't you see? After all, my boy, what good is owning something if you can't give it to someone else to appreciate?

Sometimes the greatest gifts are the ones that leave your hands empty and your heart full. Now how many times do I have to say it? Take that toy where it wants to go before the boy's too old to enjoy it! Oh... and don't forget to open the door on your way out."

"The door?" I asked in desperation. "But what door?"

"The magic door, of course," he sang out. "The one that's right in front of your nose."

And so saying, he let out one last glorious whoop and disappeared, leaving in his place a thicket of bright red roses.

I can't say exactly how long I stood there with my mouth agape before it dawned on me that he had been talking of Jaspar and the music box. How, I wondered, could he possibly have known? But then, looking down at my bundle, I realized that it hardly mattered anyway since he was absolutely right. I raced back to Jaspar's house and, tiptoeing into his room, left the music box by his side so he could enjoy it from the moment he awoke.

That afternoon, as I made my way home for the second time, I was overcome with an indescribable joy. I felt like a child who has just tasted his first snowflake. A terrific lightness quickened my pace, and as I neared my doorstep, I found myself humming a familiar tune:

Deep in seeds of giving lie
Fruit and flower of living.
The fortunate need not ask why,
It is all a matter of knowing.

Now at last I understood Elder's words — puzzle, riddle, prophecy and all. I knew then that my rightful path and my own happiness were really one and the same. If I could make gifts that brought joy to others, then I too would feel this happy forever. The answer had been in my hands all along.

And by the way, that old woodsman had spoken the truth. The music of the little carousel never played as sweetly as when it played for someone else. Its melody is still with me to this very day, and it never fails to take me back to the moment when that magic door first opened and I stepped through....

CHAPTER FIVE

The First Christmas Journey

Though it is said that every great journey begins with a single step, it just so happens that the first step is often the hardest one to make. So I learned as I began my life's voyage that it takes far more than mere wishing and wanting to make dreams come alive.

In those early days there seemed to be so much before me that I was nearly overwhelmed by the size of my task. There were countless plans to make and so many obstacles to tackle that hardly had one problem been solved before yet another arose. The only thing I was absolutely sure of was that I wanted to bring my gifts to each and every child in the village. With this thought in my mind and visions of the children in my heart, I started my work, hoping that in time all of my other questions would answer themselves, as Elder had promised.

I began simply, using a trick that my father had taught me years before, and if you'll let me, I would like to teach it to you now.

Wherever you are at this moment, simply stop and look around. You can look at the patterns in the grain of a wooden floor, if you like, or if you are sitting by a fire, watching the flames will do nicely. I've always found that clouds on a sunny day work best for me, but it's all a matter of preference. Now, once you've found something to look at, concentrate very hard, and soon you will begin to see that there are pictures in everything, even in places you might never have thought to find them. The longer you look, the more pictures you will see as the patterns move and change. The reason for this is that everything, everywhere, has a story it wants to tell, and so if you are ever stuck for an idea, all you have to do is let the world tell you its stories. The same is true for carving wood, Anselm always said, for the wood already has an idea of what it wants to be, and the finest work is done when you just let it guide your hand.

Since I didn't know where to start at first, I decided to follow his advice and simply held a block of wood in my palm until it revealed the shape of my first real toy. With the beginning strokes of my chisel, the form of an animal slowly began to emerge, and at the very heart of the wood, I discovered a beautiful little bear, so alive that the birds on my windowsill flew off in a fright.

From then on, the months flew by as I worked at my carpentry bench from dawn until long after dark, carving, sanding, and painting my toys by the bugswirled light of the oil lamps. Before long, my table was a jungle of tiny wooden creatures with polished stone eyes and legs that could bend and move. They were quickly joined by blocks and boats, tops of all sizes and little toy houses. The shelves overflowed with drums and dolls and handsome stout soldiers, painted sleds and speedy wagons and paper kites in every color.

Higher and higher grew the stacks of toys until I could barely see out of the windows. Though the days were long and the work exhausting, I must admit that I had never before had so much fun, for there wasn't a toy made that I did not stop to play with.

Seeing what a wonderful time I was having, Anselm would often break from his own work to join me at my side, adding finishing touches and suggesting new designs. Gerda, too, was eager to lend a helping hand, and she busied herself decorating the hobby horses and sewing lavish costumes for the dolls. We were all so caught up in the dream that we began to act like youngsters ourselves, laughing and chattering with excitement like children in a child's paradise.

Anselm also helped me solve the problem of how to deliver all the toys, and together we repaired the timeworn sleigh that he used for jobs in nearby villages. He even fashioned a new set of harnesses so that our faithful reindeer, Donner and Blitzen, could pull my cargo over the long miles.

As time marched on, spring turned into late summer. The toys continued to grow in number and so did my circle of helpers. My father gave word of my plan to his friends, and they all joined in, the tinsmiths and tinkers and weavers alike, donating supplies and suggestions and a brand new set of carving tools.

Just when it seemed that nothing could possibly further the joy I took in my work, I received the most wonderful surprise of all. It was an autumn afternoon and I was about to doze off at my workbench when a soft knock came on the door, and in walked my dear friend Sara, even lovelier than I remembered.

Sara lived in the neighboring village, and we had been close friends ever since childhood. In those days, we had played together in school, shared our daydreams and secret wishes, and explored the forest like proper pioneers. Once, she taught me how to mimic the songs of birds so they would come to eat from our hands. Another time, she showed me how to get fresh honey from lilac blossoms. I was always amazed at all of the unusual things she could do, and I knew even at that young age that our friendship was something special. When our school days ended, though, our lives took different paths as we both became busy with the responsibilities of adulthood. Still, we had never been far from each other's thoughts, and now here she was, come to join me in my calling.

After our joyful reunion, she emptied the contents of the sack she had brought, filling the last empty spot on the floor with bundles of yarn and brightly colored scraps of cloth.

"What you need," she announced with a wink, "are some stuffed toys in that treasure-trove of yours."

And so it came to be that Sara and I began working side by side, her calico dolls and bright cloth menagerie joining the wooden toys in the storage shed.

Well, it wasn't long before the days were growing shorter and autumn's last flowers felt the chill of the early frosts. Winter was coming, and in a matter of weeks, the snow would blanket the woodland. Christmas would soon be here too, I realized, and I could certainly deliver my gifts then. By that time I would have enough toys to give to all the children for miles around. The timing seemed almost too perfect to be coincidence. What better time could there be to make my visit to the children than this blessed season of peace and goodwill?

There is truly nothing that makes the days go faster than the sweet anticipation of something special. It's that feeling of excitement that comes with the first rumblings of a thunderstorm, or the beginning of spring, or — as you and I have both come to know so well — before the magical dawning of Christmas day. This was the kind of anticipation that I had as the last toys were painted and the final preparations were being made for my very first journey.

Once all the toys had been finished, it took us the better part of a day to gather them together, load the sleigh, and harness the anxious reindeer. Then, at long last, everything was ready to go.

As dusk announced the approach of Christmas Eve, my mother unveiled the special surprise that she had made just for the occasion: a beautiful green traveling coat the color of the forest, with leather buttons and white woolen trim. I donned the handsome suit, said my farewells, and with a crack of the reins, I sped off into the night.

Never will I forget the exhilaration of that first time — the light snow dusting the trees and the sleigh humming over the sparkling fields. And how the full moon cast our silver shadows onto the icy ground. We raced that moon long into morning, slipping silently from village to village, stopping wherever children slept to leave gifts on their doorsteps and windowsills.

Of course, my Christmas visit took much longer then, for there was much I had yet to learn about the magic of gift giving. In fact, I spent the entire week, right up until New Year's Day, traveling to all of the neighboring townships. The reindeer and I had to stay in stables along the way, and we met with such cheer and kindness everywhere that I felt as though I could go on forever. But when the first morning bells of the new year began to ring, my toybag was finally empty and I knew it was time to return home.

CHAPTER SIX
The Blizzard or How The Reindeer Got Their Wings

$\mathcal{I}$n the years that followed, my Christmas visits went much the same way, except that each time my travels took me to the children in ever more distant places. By then, the story of the secret Christmas gift-giver had become well-known throughout the land, and children everywhere had begun to expect my arrival with boundless excitement. In many of the villages the children had hung stockings on their doors so that their presents would be kept safe from prying animals — a clever idea that has remained a tradition in some places to this very day. Some eager children even tried to stay up late and find out just who this mysterious person was, but I always waited until the moment they dropped off to sleep and then, quiet as a shadow, I would leave their gifts and steal off into the night. Now, it's not that I wouldn't have loved to sit down and talk with each and every child, but with so many villages to cover, there simply would never have been enough time.

To make my trip a little easier, though, the children began to leave not only letters, but also cookies and hot cocoa. Once, a little girl drew a marvelous picture of me as she thought I looked: a giant rainbow bird leaving a trail of gifts across the night sky. I still keep that picture above my mantelpiece, and though the paper is yellowed and brittle with age, the colors haven't faded one bit. Even now, it makes me think back to that one evening when I first discovered that I had more in common with that rainbow bird than I could ever have imagined.

It was late one Christmas Eve, and I was on the first leg of my long journey, traveling through a remote stretch of tundra that lay nearly twenty miles from the nearest town. The sky had been brooding with storm clouds since nightfall, and there was neither moon nor stars to light our way. Sharp winds blew a bitter chill through my heavy coat, and Donner and Blitzen were shivering so much that the whole sleigh rattled on its runners. Sara had warned me not to go out that night, but I had to risk it; there were too many children faithfully awaiting my visit, and I couldn't let a storm stand in my way.

For a while, it seemed as though the snowstorm might not come after all, but then, late into the night, the first snowflakes began to fall. They were each as big as my palm, and they stung my bare cheeks like a swarm of icy hornets. Within minutes, so many millions of them were tumbling from the sky that I could hardly see the front of the sleigh.

As the snowdrifts piled up around us, the reindeer lowered their antlers to the frigid winds and valiantly pressed on, straining to keep the sleigh moving. The furious frost had hung my eyebrows with icicles and frozen me to my seat. At the rate we were moving, I knew there was little hope of reaching the next town; it was only a matter of time before we would have to surrender to the blizzard.

Suddenly, there came a tremendous crash, and the sleigh lurched to a standstill. I jumped out and found that we had lodged ourselves on the rocky banks of a hill. Try as I might, I could not free the sleigh, and the reindeer were too exhausted to pull any harder. Desperately, the three of us huddled together beneath the sleigh for shelter, struggling to save ourselves from this icy doom. My hands were growing numb, and the chattering of my teeth echoed throughout my frozen bones as I sank deeper and deeper into the snow. I began to think of all the children who would awaken from their dreams of Christmas wonders to find only emptiness in their stockings. Was this to be where the dream ended?

Yes, I thought, there is nothing more that we can do.

And then, from beyond the blinding shroud of snow, there came a soft, high piping — the very same melody I had heard that day at the chasm. The reindeer pricked up their ears and rose to their feet. From out of nowhere, a strange light surrounded us all in a pale fire. I sat there, motionless, praying beneath my breath that it was not a mirage.

Through the furious blizzard, above the piping, I heard again the mystical voice of Elder:

Nicholas, come seek the sky.
Beyond the clouds your dreams run free....

And then the piping ceased, as swiftly as it had begun, leaving only the laughing winds to taunt my ears.

The reindeer were standing up now, pawing at the ground. Sensing that something was about to happen, I climbed into the sleigh and groped blindly for the reins. The mysterious glow grew brighter, and the entire sleigh began to vibrate until every bolt and peg sang out. Then, ever so slowly, we slid from the rocks, and as we moved toward the snow-swept fields, I was struck by a curious thought: Why did the trees seem to be getting smaller?

That was when I realized that instead of moving forward, or indeed in any direction a sleigh ought to have gone, the reindeer and I were rising straight up into the air.

Too terror-stricken to watch, I covered my eyes with a shaky hand and ducked down beneath my seat as the winds howled around us. Up and further up we soared, right through the very heart of the storm until we reached the clear night sky above. It was only then that I first dared to look, and, peering over the front of the sleigh, my eyes were filled with the miraculous twinkling beauty of starlight.

Oh, how I whooped and hollered that night! Why, I almost tumbled out of the sleigh with all of my joyous leaping and dancing. Even the reindeer frolicked and frisked through the sky like fawns in a field of starry clover.

Never has there been a tale of magic carpets or flying ships that could compare to the marvels of that first flight. All about us there drifted vapor mists of unknown colors, and above our heads the constellations swam through the dark night sea. The moon's broad smile shone more brightly than ever before, and she blew us all a kiss as we passed. High above that blustery blizzard we sailed, lighter even than spider's silk, until we spotted a village of tiny pin-sized houses through a clearing in the clouds. As though they had guessed my thoughts, Donner and Blitzen were already guiding the sleigh back down to our destination.

Through the clouds we sped, the streets and rooftops growing nearer until I could see the colors of each window shutter and trace the cobblestone paths to every door. As gently as a leaf landing on water, the sleigh touched down in the village square. The blizzard had quieted considerably, and now only a soft flurry was left to cover my footprints as I crept from house to house. Then, with the children's stockings all filled, I hopped back into the sleigh, and in a wink, we took to the skies again, heading for the next stop. Throughout the night we soared on unseen wings, and the long miles melted away beneath us with such speed that by the first rays of daybreak the gifts had all been delivered and we were on our way home.

But I didn't go directly home that morning; I simply couldn't until I had shared the story of this fantastic adventure with the one person I longed to see most, and that person was Sara. Straight to her cottage we flew, only this time our landing was not quite as smooth, and we ended up inside her barn, much to the distress of the dozing cows.

By the time I had dusted myself off and picked the hay from my trousers, Sara was at the barn door, still bundled in her bedclothes with her hair done up in braids. She greeted me with a big hug and then sat with my hand in hers, wide-eyed as I told her the details of my extraordinary evening. When I had finally finished, she just smiled and said:

"The world is filled with miracles, Nicholas. They happen all the time, especially when you least expect them...."

And with that, she gave me a kiss that melted the frost on my toes. Well, she looked so lovely and I was so overjoyed that I could contain myself no longer, and right then and there, among the bales of hay and snoring cows, I asked if she would be my wife....

And of course she said yes, or I wouldn't be telling you this part of the story, now would I?

CHAPTER SEVEN

The Snow Gryphon

*T*he wedding took place that spring, and it was an occasion so magnificent that the village storytellers have told of it ever since. The celebration lasted through the day and on into the following afternoon, with all of the villagers and all of their children dancing until they shook the hills. Drummers and fiddlers and minstrels from the northernmost reaches came and played their legendary instruments without once pausing for breath. There were jugglers and acrobats, jesters in animal costumes and fire-eaters who could swallow the flames and spit them back in the most dazzling array of colors.

Most of all, there was the feast — and oh what a feast that was! One great oaken table, as long as twenty men, laden beyond possibility with fine fruits and cheeses and long loaves of bread, kettles of stew and barrels of sweet honey wine; licorice puddings and gooseberry pies and tremendous cakes fit for storybook giants.

So bright and merry were the festivities that the wilting spring flowers all bloomed again, bigger and more magnificent than before. Even when the darkness came, the night sky was alight with the wondrous colored fireworks that the merchants had brought back from the East.

And then, when the last of the revelers had gone off to rest and Sara and I thought we were alone, we heard strange murmurs beckoning to us from the forest. We followed their call until we reached a wide clearing where, in the center, we found our parents, standing before the most wonderful gift of all: a beautiful new house, built by the hands of each and every villager. It had the grandest stained-glass windows beneath its high peaked roofs, its very own workshop in the back, and from the topmost room, we could see the very same waterfalls where the whole tale had begun.

Our new life together brought constant happiness to both of us and made our toys ever more enchanting with each passing year. It was around this time, too, that my beard began to grow, along with my famous belly (but that is another matter), and I started to look a little more like the fellow you might recognize today. In any case, with Sara's help in the workshop, I even learned to weave my own cloth and stitch fine stuffed animals and soft rag dolls. Of course, my life was not devoted solely to working, and I still made certain to enjoy quiet walks in the forest when I needed to be inspired.

Walking on a winter afternoon, I've found, is the best time just to listen. If you are very quiet and don't speak a word, you might hear the squirrels arguing over their acorns. Or perhaps you might hear the sounds of icicles forming, or the snow settling to the ground, or the unmistakable toc-toc-toc of the woodpecker feasts. What you most likely will never hear on a winter afternoon (though be sure to proceed with caution if you do) is the dreadful cry of the sad and wretched snow gryphon. But that, as you may have guessed, was exactly the terrible, awful, bone-rattling sound that I heard on a January morning many years ago.

I couldn't imagine where such a creature had come from, but there was no mistaking that it most certainly was there — as big as the biggest bear and nearly twice as long, with a gleaming beak and sharp talons and two tremendous wings that beat the snow into a furious squall. Its white feathered body looked just like that of an enormous frost-covered bird, except for the long scaly lizard's tail that was the source of its distress, for it was pinned firmly beneath a heavy fallen tree. To make matters worse, the beast lay trapped directly on the only path back to my home, leaving me no choice but to draw nearer. Upon seeing me, it swung its massive head about and let out a piercing screech as gusts of bitter frost blew forth from its nostrils. And then, incredibly, a single frozen tear fell from the corner of one eye and shattered on the ground. The creature was crying.

At first I thought that it might have been a trick, for I had heard many a tale of devious serpents who shed false tears, only to devour their would-be rescuers. But there was something about this creature, terrible though it was, that quickly turned my horror to pity. It might have been the baleful droop of its eyes or the almost human sound beneath its moan. Or perhaps it was simply that I couldn't bear the thought of anything suffering so. Whatever the reason, though, I knew for certain that I could not leave the beast to such a fate.

Quick as a wink, I scrambled behind it, careful to avoid the fearsome talons, and gathered up the necessary materials for a makeshift lever. For the better part of the afternoon I pulled and pushed and sweated and strained, while the creature wailed in

pain, yet I could not budge the heavy tree trunk. Finally, nearly at my wit's end, I had an idea: using a trick that Sara had taught me, I called together all of the nearby beavers and termites and carpenter ants, and set them to work. In a brief flurry of flying splinters, they devoured the tree trunk, and the creature was free.

And then a most extraordinary thing happened: rearing up on its hind legs, the creature spread its wings and began to grow. Within moments, its tremendous size had dwarfed the pines and blotted the sun from view. I covered my eyes and crouched trembling in the underbrush while the air all about me was split with an ominous rumble and a deafening shriek, followed by nothing but silence.

When I looked up again, the towering beast was gone, and in its place, beneath a wreath of blue smoke, there stood a tiny man. He sported a trim gray beard and twinkling eyes, and in his sharp green suit and yellow cap he looked like a dandelion gone mad. With hardly a pause, he doffed his cap and spoke:

"Oh most wonderful, honorable, praiseworthy man! A thousand thanks be to you, kind sir, for now I am free as a bird, fit as a fiddle, happy as a lark, and quite as right as rain!"

"But...but...who...?" I stammered, quite astonished.

"Tut!" he interrupted. "All in good time and all time is good, so listen and you will understand."

"But who are you and where did you come from?" I blurted out at last.

With a little hint of impatience, the imp snapped his fingers beneath my nose and vanished, only to reappear atop my head, where he began a little dance:

Behoove me if you will, kind sir;
For I'm known as many things.
From will-o-wisp
To whippoorwill
To the church bell when it rings.
(And many's the time that I have sat
on the thrones of Aztec kings.)

I'm the sounds you often hear at night,
I'm the things you can't explain,
Like walls with ears
And flying deers
And why the weather's vain.
(And if you ask me, I'll be glad
to cure your window's pain.)

If you insist, you'll get the gist,
Of where I've been and why.
But that, I say,
Could take all day,
And evening's drawing nigh.
(Although I will continue
if you feel that you must pry.)

I've whooped with all the whooping cranes
And slept inside a drop of rain.
I've won the hearts of ladybugs,
And drunk from jugs with wild slugs,
Who roam the northern plain.
(And as for all the world's white sand,
I've counted every grain.)

Now I don't mean to boast,
But I have been host
To sultans, caliphs, and czars,
Who dined on figs and cold earwigs
And lizards from Zanzibar.
(With dragonfly wine, they're simply divine,
though they do taste a little like tar.)

And just last week, I met a sheik
On an isle of cinnamon tea,
Where the princesses there go
To the oyster concerto,
Beneath the Sargasso sea.

(And mermaids in curls mix a potion of pearls,
which they'll serve for a minimal fee.)

Yes, I've hung from the gardens of Babylon,
Where the peacocks all sing the same tune.
And it's even been heard,
Though I won't say a word,
That I've danced on the sands of the moon.
(But the green cheese up there is beyond compare,
so be sure to bring your own spoon.)

I could tell you long tales of the old toothless Yeti
Or the laughing giraffes of the broad Serengeti
But sir! Now I see you're beginning to tire.
Then I'll stop here instead,
For the fibs you've been fed
Are the work of a fabulous liar.

Yes, the man now before you
(And I speak of myself)
Is really none other than a mischievous elf,
A member, 'tis true, of the kind elfin clan,
That dwells with old Elder in the deep forest land.
Please, sir, don't be nervous,
For I am, at your service,
Giraldus, the Masterman.

And with that, he leapt from my head and took a courtly bow.

"Well done! Truly magnificent!" I said, applauding him heartily. "But you still haven't explained what became of that creature I freed but a moment ago."

"Oho and Aha!" Giraldus replied, clearly delighted with the prospect of a tale to tell. "That, sir, is another story entirely."

And so, perching upon a branch like a big green and yellow spider, the Masterman began to weave his web of words...

CHAPTER EIGHT
The Masterman's Tale

*I*n the time before time and the time after that, when the sun was silver and the flowers grew tall as the trees, this earth was a very different place indeed. So different, in fact, that you humans were still just animals of the forest, and we fairy folk dwelt peacefully in the great kingdom of Elfhame. Presiding over all the elfin tribes was our wise and all-seeing leader, the beloved Elder (yes, yes, the very same one, but don't interrupt); he alone knew the secrets of the Pipes of Power, that wondrous warbling birdsong of peace.

I myself, being as I was the Masterman of the Favored Elves, was a fellow of no little importance, if I do say so. We were a large and good-hearted tribe, gifted in the ways of the natural world. It was up to us to make certain that the leaves turned their proper colors in autumn (the red ones were my idea, I'll have you know), *not to mention freezing the lakes in winter and seeing that the animals behaved like animals should. Of course, there was always time for plenty of mischief, but never, to be sure, with a single unkind thought, for even our quarrels were had in good humor.*

And so it remained for centuries on end, all manner of creatures rejoicing in their harmony, innocent of the wickedness to come. But then, oh my brother, in the year the stars fell to earth, all the trouble began.

It was on a quiet summer's evening, those lazy stars falling this way and that, that a stranger appeared among us; a most dour old elf he was, with a face like a nutcracker and a band of nasty looking hobgoblins at his heels. His name was Hoarfrost, he told us, and he claimed to be a poor wandering shepherd in search of a lost flock, and could he, he wondered, rest with us for a bit until he found his sheep?

Well, unsavory though he and his cohorts did seem, it was most unthinkable to turn anyone away from our land, so we welcomed him without question. After that first evening, though, no one ever saw him by daylight again, and since he never joined us in feasting or games, we soon forgot about him altogether. That, as we would quickly learn, turned out to be a dreadful mistake.

It really all began with the turnips, you see — more turnips than anybody (or anything else for that matter) could ever imagine. Turnips, in fact, were all that grew that year, and it seemed as if they would never stop growing. Where there had once been corn and beans and melons, now there was nothing but turnips. Berry patches yielded turnips by the bushelfull, and instead of apples on the apple trees, what do you think we found? Turnips! No matter how many times we yanked them out and tossed them away, up they came again, bigger and fatter, all waxy-white and purple.

As you may have guessed by now, there is nothing — and I mean nothing — that an elf likes less than that horrid vegetable. Now, pumpkins are delectable and beets quite a treat, and even parsnips will do in a pinch, but never had a turnip been any more than a bothersome old weed! Yet there they were and they were everywhere, and that's all there was to eat.

Day and night we ate those awful things in turnip stew and turnip bread, pickled turnips and turnip roast. We ate them and ate them until we were white in the face and purple all around, and we had to build ourselves a great big cider press just to squeeze the turnip juice out of us. Eventually, we all simply chose to eat nothing at all, and so we soon became the scrawniest, sickliest bunch that you ever did see. No longer was there time for the games and merrymaking of old. Terrible fights began to break out over any morsel that was not a turnip, and we quickly plunged into utter chaos.

And then — oh ragweed and bitters! — as if that was not a miserable enough fate, we soon were to discover that it was only the tip of the turnip. That, oh Brother Nicholas, was when the ravens came.

At first, there were just a few little incidents of missing objects and scritch-scratch noises in the night, but when the ravens began to turn up in our closets and under our beds, we knew they meant business! Where they had come from, nobody knew, but suddenly there was no escaping the sound of their soot-black wings. Down, down from the sky they came each and every evening to peer through our windows with their fiery red eyes and tread on our rooftops with their horrible feet. They scratched at our doors while we huddled in fear, and they kept us awake with their awful, terrible cries: Screeeeawwwk! Arrraawwwk! Screeeeawwwk!

It was enough to drive us out of our minds, and after weeks of little food or sleep, that is practically what it did. Our playful squabbles soon turned into long bitter feuds, and we couldn't even leave our homes for fear of our own shadows. Yet still the ravens persisted until at last I could stand it no longer. Something had to be done to put an end to the misery, so I thought up a plan and I thought it up quick:

Those ravens were known to be shameless thieves, so I placed a shiny brass urn on my doorstep and hid myself inside it, waiting until nightfall — quite brave of me, don't you think? Well, surely enough, when the sky grew dark, the ravens returned, and one, spotting the fabulous urn, seized it in its talons and carried me with it up into the air. At length, when I found myself set back on the ground, I peered through the lid of the urn, only to find myself right in the center of the fetid nettle bogs, surrounded on all sides by heaps of gold and glittering jewels.

Late that night, I made a most fascinating discovery. The ravens, as it turned out, weren't ravens at all, for as each one fluttered to the ground, their forms changed to reveal none other than Hoarfrost's greedy hobgoblins. From my hiding place, I watched in horror as they feasted on caterpillars and skunk cabbage, talking loudly of their evil plot. I learned that the worst was still yet to come. The turnips and ravens were only meant to frustrate and confuse us while Hoarfrost's vile henchmen carried out his real scheme: to steal Elder's glorious Pipes of Power. Oh how those foul creatures laughed at their own wickedness — I shudder to think of it even now.

Then, as my luck would have it, the hobgoblins soon fell to arguing over the night's spoils, and as they knocked each other on the head with sticks, I slipped off to warn Elder of the terrible danger.

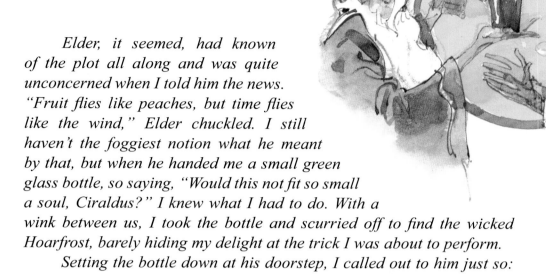

Elder, it seemed, had known of the plot all along and was quite unconcerned when I told him the news. "Fruit flies like peaches, but time flies like the wind," Elder chuckled. I still haven't the foggiest notion what he meant by that, but when he handed me a small green glass bottle, so saying, "Would this not fit so small a soul, Ciraldus?" I knew what I had to do. With a wink between us, I took the bottle and scurried off to find the wicked Hoarfrost, barely hiding my delight at the trick I was about to perform.

Setting the bottle down at his doorstep, I called out to him just so: "Oh most excellent Hoarfrost, I am pleased to hear of the news of your great plans. That old ninny Elder's time has come, it is true, but who is to say that you are worthy to take his place? If you are truly the sorcerer that you claim, then let me see you climb into this bottle, a feat that even Elder cannot do. If you succeed where he has failed, then I know that you deserve to be our rightful leader."

Now, you may ask yourself why anyone would ever agree to such a ridiculous thing, but you must understand that it is one of the unwritten rules of Elfhame that no elf can ever resist another's challenge. Thus, needless to say, the haughty Hoarfrost leapt into the bottle without a second thought, and quick as a cricket's wink, I stoppered it up and trapped him inside. No matter how he ranted and raved and stamped his feet, he could do nothing to free himself. And so, slipping him into my pocket, I brought the evildoer to stand judgment before the Great Autumnal Council.

75

The trial was short but fair, and all present agreed to let Hoarfrost's fate match the coldness of his heart. From that day forth, he was to be banished to the vast frozen reaches where the night is without end and where only the winter's chill would be his companion. As for the hobgoblins, well, they were sentenced to join him, and to eat all of the remaining turnips until their teeth fell out.

When the judgment had been passed down, our beloved Elder raised high his hands, and down from the sky there flew a flock of giant snowy owls, come to carry away the evildoers. As he and his loathsome cronies were borne aloft, the black-hearted Hoarfrost uttered poisoned curses upon my head, vowing to someday take his revenge.

Well, I suppose there must have been a leak in the stopper of that bottle, for in the dark of night a hideous transformation took place while I slept. Come morning, I awoke to find myself trapped in the body of that terrible snow gryphon you happened upon this very day. Nigh a thousand moons did I endure that wretched fate, chased from my home and shunned even by the insects, who ran in fear from my ugliness.

But you, gentle Toymaker, you have shown kindness such as I thought I never would see. For that, I shall end my tale with the giving of a gift. Now it is time to return to your home, for when the roosters crow at dawn, you shall find there what you deserve.

CHAPTER NINE

Gifts From The Forest

Inch time tin toe
Up we come and
down we go.

Nail all the nails
And polish the floors,
And let's not forget
To leave room for the doors.

With footsteps of spiders,
As quiet as sheep,
We'll build ever higher
While the Toymaker sleeps.

And when the sun shines,
It's a marvelous thing,
To raise high the roofbeams
And build while we sing:

Inch time tin toe
Up we come and down we go.

With one thousand hammers
And five hundred saws,
Like carpenter ants
With carpenter's claws.

We'll tile the rooftops
And seal all the seams.
We'll make the dream toys
From the Toymaker's dreams.

And the bees in the glade
And the crows on the wing,
All pause for a dance
To the song that we sing:

Inch time tin toe
Up we come and down we go....

So went the song that greeted my ears as I awoke from my dreams early the next morning. Pressing my sleepy face to the bedroom window, I discovered the singers of the song right in my own backyard, scurrying around what looked like an enormous new building. But it couldn't be, I thought, for buildings don't simply sprout up like weeds in the night. Then again, I never would have believed that reindeer could fly until I flew them myself, so unless I was dreaming, this magnificent structure was perfectly real.

I sat back down in bed, gave my whiskers a sharp tug to be sure I was awake and peered through the frosted glass of the window once again.

No, I definitely wasn't dreaming; the building was still there, and what's more, there were also hundreds of tiny elves in yellow and green, indigo, crimson and purple, bustling this way and that, their brilliant colors speckling the snow like a bunch of wildflowers. They came in all shapes and sizes (well, all sizes of small to be exact), some bearded and some bejeweled, some with caps and others bareheaded, all of them singing and all of them, both male and female, young and old, were just as giddy as bees in the springtime.

Being careful not to awaken Sara, I slipped out of the bedroom and crept outside to examine this glorious spectacle.

"Master Nicholas! Master Nicholas! Over here!"

Through the flurry of jostling limbs and scurrying bodies, I spotted the grinning face of my new friend Giraldus, calling out my name as though we had known each other for a lifetime.

"Welcome to your new workshop, Toymaker," he beamed, racing over to squeeze my hand and dance on my feet. "Come along with me, and I'll introduce you to your new family!"

"New workshop? My new family?" I asked, more than a bit puzzled. "What's this all about, Giraldus?"

"Oh really, Master Nick," he answered. "With all due respect, sir, you mustn't be so beetleheaded, it simply doesn't become you. Now take a look around — these elves are to be your family just as they have been mine. Each one of them with a skill unparalleled, and ready to use it as you please." As he said this, he pointed to the chattering horde of elves who were busy fitting handles on the windows and knobs on the doors.

"I told you that you would find what you deserve, yes I did, and here you have it! We've come to join you in your work, Toymaker, so let's get right to it. Now follow me and I'll show you what's what."

On our way into the building, Ciraldus was a blur of gestures and announcements, pointing out the countless elves as we passed them by. There were tree elves and river elves, weed elves next to garden elves, drowsy daydream elves and bright color elves. There were elves for songs and elves for secrets, elves for riddles and elves for speeches (both the short and long kind). There were so many different sorts of them that my head began to swim — which, I suspect, was the fault of the head-swimming elves.

"As you can see," said Giraldus proudly, "there is an elf for everything. We're the ones who keep the world in its proper order — a thankless task, you say, and a thankless task even if you don't say. Why, we even have elves in charge of nasty habits and not-so-pleasant smells. We never leave a stone unturned; the stone-turning elves see to that. As I always say, there wouldn't be selves without elves."

"What are those?" I asked, pointing to a rather shady bunch of characters lurking in the doorway.

"Those are the shadow elves, of course. Who do you think follows you around from sunup to sundown?"

I must admit I'd never thought of it before, but then I was quickly learning that most things are rarely quite what they appear to be. As we continued on, we passed another group of elves who, I noticed, bore a striking resemblance to myself.

"Those," said Giraldus, without being asked, "are the reflection elves. They're very good mimics, you know. But come on now, we mustn't dawdle or dally. You can see them anytime in any mirror or rain puddle. They always know where you are."

"But I thought..." I began, only to be interrupted by a tiny voice from my left ear.

"Thought! A thought is no more than an itch on your brain!"

"That's right!" chimed in a second voice into the other ear. "Why do you suppose everyone always runs about saying, 'Scratch that thought! Scratch that thought!'"

Both voices promptly broke out into great hiccups of laughter, tickled silly by their own joke.

"Gerhombus! Gerundus! You come down from there right now!" barked my guide sternly. Immediately, two elves clad all in blue came clambering down from either shoulder, trying their best to look innocent.

"Please pay no attention to them, Master Nick," said Giraldus. "They're just the Ratchets in the Works — always looking for trouble."

He frowned at the two imps and then scooted them off with instructions to bring forth the High Toy Command. In no time at all, they reappeared with five others in tow. One by one, the little fellows nudged their way to the front and graciously introduced themselves by name:

"Pleased, charmed, delighted, and honored!" said the first from beneath a purple cap that covered his face. "I am Estivus, Supreme Overseer of Operations — the right-hand man of your right-hand man and ready to avail, advantage, aid, and assist your every need!"

"Lapidus," piped in the stony-faced second, "Mason High Superior, if you please." (The elves, as I soon discovered, simply love those fancy titles — everybody gets one.)

"Jarvis, good Master Nicholas," said a paint-spattered elf, extending a paint-spattered hand. "Head Color-Mixer Deluxe, at your disposal."

"I'm Hibernius, to be sure," rasped the husky fourth fellow, "Most Special Whittier Extraordinaire."

"Pickled tink! Oh dear, no, I mean... pinkled tick!" fumbled the fifth, blushing the color of his petunia-pink suit. "That is... oh fumf! Happy to make your acquaintance, kind sir. I'm Junius, Chief Master Smithy at sore yervice… er, your service."

With the introductions completed, Giraldus clapped his hands, and the elves scurried off every which way. The Masterman then took hold of my arm and led me at last into the cavernous halls of what was to be my new workshop. Already there was so much to see inside that glorious place, and it was growing larger with every step.

On and on we walked, past whittling benches and weaving chambers, rumbling conveyor belts and bottomless storage bins; through sanding rooms that smelled of the seashore and painting rooms covered top to bottom with golden faucets, one for every color of the rainbow and beyond. There were inventing rooms and playing rooms, viewing rooms and growing rooms, gently bending elbow rooms, and soft, spongy mushrooms. There was even an

enormous kitchen with great big burbling cauldrons of chocolate and spun sugar, where the Confectioner Elves made splendid candied fruits and flowers. I could have spent a year in there alone, had not Giraldus insisted on leading me into what appeared to be a long row of stables.

In the center, there stood the silhouette of a magnificent reindeer — proud and strong and somehow strangely familiar. As if in answer to my unspoken wonder, the young buck stepped forward and turned his head to one side, revealing the marking of the morning star on his left ear. I knew in that instant that this was none other than that very same fawn I had rescued from the chasm so many years before.

"It would appear that you and Prancer have already been acquainted, have you not?" said Giraldus with an audible grin.

"Indeed we have," I replied as I greeted my old friend. "But then I suppose you know all about it, don't you?"

"Oh, perhaps I do and perhaps I don't. All I know for certain is that things do happen for a reason. Just ask Prancer."

"What's this 'Prancer' business, Giraldus? And isn't it about time you stopped being so mysterious?"

"I am an elf, Master Nick, and I must uphold my reputation. Besides, Prancer is his name, of course. He told me himself. They all did."

"And just who might 'they' be?" I asked with a mock sigh.

Giraldus whistled loudly, and from out of the wooden stalls there appeared five more majestic reindeer, each as fine and strong as the one before it. Leaping from one to the other, the Masterman proceeded to sing out their names in his usual elfish manner:

There's Comet, so swift that he lights up the sky,
And Cupid, the one with the gleam in his eye,
And Dasher, as bold as the stouthearted willows,
While Vixen plays tricks on each one of his fellows.
There's Dancer, as graceful and light as a bird,
And lastly, there's Prancer, whose star says the word,
For he is the leader,
This fabulous creature,
The prince of the star-blazing, cloud-grazing herd.

"We found them in the forest just this morning," the Masterman continued, with a wink. "They have come to help Donner and Blitzen carry your new Christmas cargo. Things are going to be a bit different with us around here, you know."

And so it was, indeed. Sara and I had grown so accustomed to the peace and quiet of our lives together that I was certain it might take some time to adjust to the hustle-bustle racket of our new companions. But she was so delighted with their antics, and I with their imaginations and exceptional skills, that I soon grew to wonder how we had ever managed without them.

In almost no time at all, the elves had settled themselves into the new workshop and were turning out toys the likes of which the world had never seen. There were humming-tops and colored glass marbles, clockwork dolls and rainbow spectacles, bubbles and baubles and battle-board games. There were even mysterious magic tricks for aspiring illusionists and marvelous instruments for tiny tot symphonies.

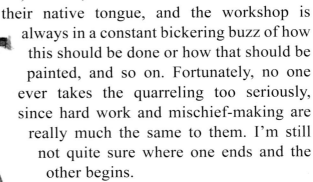

Many were the delirious evenings that we spent crowded together in the Inventing Room, drawing up plans, showing off new designs and arguing, quibbling, and squabbling. The elves, of course, were far better at the arguing than I — it is, in fact, their native tongue, and the workshop is always in a constant bickering buzz of how this should be done or how that should be painted, and so on. Fortunately, no one ever takes the quarreling too seriously, since hard work and mischief-making are really much the same to them. I'm still not quite sure where one ends and the other begins.

I'll tell you one thing, though, they can cause quite a stir when they really set their minds to it! I've seen toy soldiers suddenly spring to life to wage war on a nearby workbench, and mechanical birds that come to roost in the open mouths of dozing workers. And many are the unfortunate elves who have found themselves glued fast to their seats or dangling from the rafters on marionette strings. Even the older, more dignified elves, the very same ones who pretend to shun these antics, often get in on the act in secret, proving themselves time and again to be the craftiest of the lot.

Once — and this was the only time I'd ever seen them at it myself — I spied a trio of these not-so-venerable oldsters hidden in the storeroom, blowing tremendous soap bubbles that swallowed up their hapless victims and sent them floating up into the rafters. I would have caught them red-handed, too, if only I hadn't given myself away with a fit of laughter. In the blink of an eye, the culprits had disappeared while somehow the incriminating bubble pipes found their way into my pockets. Yes, life with the elves was different all right, but somehow it made just enough crazy sense to keep things running smoothly. Together, we worked faster than I had ever dreamed possible, filling up the storerooms with toys enough for all the world and then some.

Sara, meanwhile, had busied herself teaching the Master Seamstress Elves a few tricks of the trade, in return for learning the secret art of turning spider's silk into cloth. Thanks to their work, I acquired a brand new red traveling suit (the very same kind that I've worn ever since), all trimmed with white wool and with trousers to match. They also wove a magical new toybag that could hold any amount of toys without ever getting any heavier than when it was empty.

All of my new gifts made the Yuletide journey that year an evening of unmatched splendors. With those eight magnificent reindeer as my steeds, we traveled faster and farther than ever before, chasing the sunsets around one half of the world and the sunrises back around the other. If you had been with me that night, you would have heard me hollering like a loon as we soared above the mists of the oceans. And had you asked me what the shouts were for, I would have told you that they were for you and me and for the joy of all the things that were only just beginning.

CHAPTER TEN
Time and Tide

*Y*ou know, when you stop to think about it, memory seems by far the most clever teller of time. While our eyes and ears wait for the ticking clocks and tolling bells to mark our days, our memories have much more interesting ways of measuring time's passage. After all, isn't it easier to remember how you felt when you first saw a shooting star than to recall what you felt like at noon yesterday? For me, being around as long as I have, I find that I remember times gone by in terms of the different toys that have filled my sleigh.

Over the many years that followed the arrival of the elves, we made gifts for the children of the ever-changing times. Our storerooms soon were filled with such delights as roller skates and pogo sticks, jigsaw puzzles and backgammon boards, chemistry sets and fancy play costumes. In time, these were joined by steam locomotives with miles of tracks, wristwatches and talking dolls and — one of my personal favorites — magic lanterns that cast moving pictures upon the walls. Then, by the days of electric lights, we began to build little automobiles with tooting horns, phonographs and windup toy airplanes, kaleidoscopes, gyroscopes, telescopes and microscopes — but now I've gotten far ahead of myself. In any case, even in our earliest days, we had come quite a long way indeed from those first wooden animals with their polished stone eyes. Now, children the world over could hold in their hands the making of their most secret dreams.

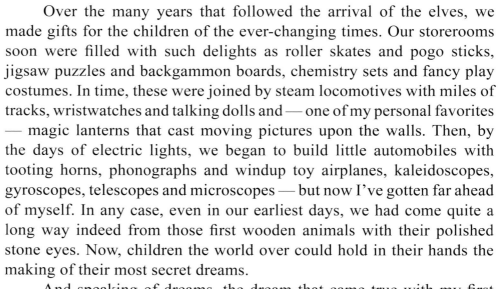

And speaking of dreams, the dream that came true with my first journey around the world was one that I'd had ever since I was a young child, back in the days when explorers still braved long and perilous sea voyages. You see, I often dreamt of traveling to all the fabulous places I had seen in picture books and fairy tales. I used to imagine sailing to Persia with Sinbad the Sailor, or riding astride the elephants of India, like Daju, the man who could smell the moon. Stories like these filled my mind with thoughts of great adventures, but never did I dare to think that one day I, too, would see all of the wondrous sights the world has to offer. But now that my Christmas visits took me as far as England and Ethiopia, Germany and Japan, I discovered Yuletide celebrations as diverse as the people who celebrate them.

Imagine Christmas surrounded by the banana trees of South America, where it never snows in winter and the air is loud with the chatter of talking parrots. Or France, where the houses from Paris to Provence are dressed all in mistletoe and holly, and the tables bend low with the nuts and candies and endless delights of the feast of the thirteen desserts (and I must admit, dear reader, that I've sampled my fair share of those goodies on many a Joyeux Noël). In Spain, I've traded a step or two with the flamenco dancers (when I was not quite so round in the middle, that is), while music and song filled the streets for the Noche-Buena celebrations.

I remember, too, the first time I saw the townships of Sri Lanka aglow with lanterns and torches and bonfires, and the people there who joined together to dance to the beating of Christmas drums. In Nigeria, I've watched as the night sky explodes with a hundred thousand colors of the Yuletide fireworks, and I've even flown above the volcanoes of Hawaii, where December is as hot as July and orchids perfume the air of the outdoor feasts.

In Mexico, I've seen weeks of revelry that would exhaust even my hardiest elves. There, in the petal-strewn streets, vendors sell candies and nuts at every corner as the children dance beneath the warm winter sun. Even the windows and doorways are hung with bright Christmas pinatas, just waiting to be burst open to share their sweetmeats and whistles and toys. In fact, it was down at the very southern tip of Mexico where I first got the idea for the Christmas tree.

It all began as I was delivering my gifts to the homes of a sunny seaside village when I happened across a curious sight. In front of one of the houses, a number of colorful fruits and peppers had been set out to dry on the boughs of a little pine tree. All those shapes and colors looked so beautiful that it seemed the perfect place to leave my gifts, and so I did, spreading them out beneath the ornamented branches. I was so pleased with the result that I went back to all the other houses and decorated their trees myself with colored paper and bits of tinsel and tiny toys. Everywhere I went that night, I did the same to all the little trees I could find, delighted with how amazed the children would be to discover such beautiful sights in the morning.

Well, I guess the idea must have caught on, because by the very next Christmas, people all over the world were decorating trees themselves, and singing songs of thanks to their beauty. Pretty soon, folks began to bring the trees inside and dress them up, some with candies and shiny glass balls and others with candles or strings of popcorn and berries. Ever since the day of that lucky discovery, Christmas trees have become one of my very favorite traditions and have lit the way for countless carolers as they spread their Yuletide cheer.

But the Christmas tree was not the only thing to come from my world travels, for these journeys brought me some of my most memorable experiences — like the one which forever changed my way of giving gifts.

It was late one Christmas Eve in a small hamlet by the Black Sea, and the angry North Winds had come to challenge me to a duel of wits. They brought with them an icy rain which had been falling steadily throughout the night and had made everything in the tiny hamlet look as though it were made of glass. This alone would not have been so bad, except that it left me without a place

to leave my gifts. There was not a single stocking waiting for me on any of the doors, and I certainly couldn't leave the presents on the doorstep or beneath a tree, or they would be ruined by the wind and freezing rain.

Peering through several windows, I noticed that the children had hung all their stockings inside by the fireplace to thaw. If I had only been able to get inside, there would have been no problems, but each house was locked up tight as a drum and neither doorways nor windows would permit my entrance. I retreated to the sleigh for a moment and sank deep in thought, while the rain continued to make the houses look like crystal palaces. As I considered my choices, I realized that there was no way I could wait for the rainstorm to end, or I would never have time to finish my rounds. At the same time, I couldn't simply leave these children without any gifts.

So there I was, caught in a conundrum and quickly turning into an icicle, when a commotion from the reindeer caught my attention. They had all begun tugging at their harness, antlers gesturing toward the rooftops. Of course — the chimneys! Maybe I could slip in through the chimneys, I thought. It seemed worth a try and was certainly better than nothing, so why not?

I snapped the reins and up we went, alighting atop the first house. With my bag slung over my back, I crept toward the chimney and peered inside, only to find that a fire was burning in the fireplace below. Even if I had been able to squeeze down the narrow passage, there was no way I could avoid burning the Christmas gifts and becoming a Christmas roast myself — and that simply would not do. I was at a standstill once again. And then I smelled it.

Something more than cold and rain was traveling
on the wind; it was the smell of sweet poppies, followed
by the unmistakable piping of that mystic minstrel, Elder.
Then, like a snake charmer's serpent, swaying and swirling to
the piping, a whirlwind of snow and ice arose in the distance. Across the
rooftops it danced a rushing, whirling, whistling dance, mysteriously
disturbing nothing in its wake. Closer it came, onto the roof where
I stood, playfully ruffling the reindeer as it passed and finally
coming to rest atop the chimney, where it hummed like a top.
Then, without warning, the snowspout dipped down
and lifted me up, toys and all, dropping me straight
down into the fire. Columns of bright sparks swirled
around me as I floated downward through the
flickering flames and glowing embers,
magically feeling no heat as I passed.

The next thing I knew, there I was, my toys still in hand, with five empty stockings peering up at me like baby birds waiting to be fed. Gathering my wits as best I could, I filled the stockings to the very top and waited to see what would happen next.

The little house was silent but for the insistent hum of the snowspout in the fireplace, and I knew that my decision had already been made for me. With a deep breath, I stepped back into the chimney and rose up as gently as woodsmoke until I was once again atop the roof. In a delightful daze, I climbed aboard the sleigh, and the team sprang into the air, quickly alighting upon the next house, where the whirlwind lay in wait.

From rooftop to rooftop and chimney to chimney we went, accompanied all the way by the snowspout's quietly humming magic. It stayed with us throughout the journey and for many years thereafter, until finally I learned its secrets well enough to enter any house on my own — even those without any chimneys.

That night, as I returned home from my incredible voyage, I was aware that I had begun to see the world with new eyes, and that the world I saw was one of neverending discoveries and infinite possibilities. And though every year brought with it many changes, the one thing that remained the same was that there were always gifts to be given and children to cherish them.

CHAPTER ELEVEN
In The Garden of Wishing Trees

By the time my belly was growing big and round and the long, silvery hairs of my beard had earned me the nickname Father Christmas, a whole generation of children had grown up knowing the wonders of my yearly visits. Now it was coming time for them to have children of their own and start the cycle anew. The elves and I decided that it would be fitting to celebrate the occasion with something truly special — something completely unique to delight the children of the new era. Together we thought long and hard and for many a day, but our efforts met with little success. We needed inspiration.

It was just about then, and not by coincidence we would come to learn, that word of a fantastic new material began to spread like wildfire among the elves. No one knew how the rumor began (which is, I suppose, the nature of rumors), but soon even the most stodgy old curmudgeons were abuzz with talk of the miraculous stuff.

According to the story, a magical clay had been discovered far to the north, where the glaciers began; a clay that had the extraordinary power to give life to anything made from it. Just thinking of all the things we could make with that clay, our imaginations were sent spinning: animals that could wag their tails and come when you called; trees that would grow without water or soil; baby dolls just like the real thing! The possibilities were endless — why, the toys would practically make themselves!

Sara and I were sure that it was the answer to all our wildest dreams. In fact, the only ones not caught up in the magic-clay fever were Estivus and Giraldus. On the day that I was preparing to make my journey north, the two skeptics decided to air their concerns.

"Oh Master Nicholas!" said Estivus, worriedly fraying the ends of his beard. "Why not let us go instead? I fear it is all just a flim, a flam, a fable and a fib!"

"That's right!" piped in Giraldus. "Listen to reason, sir. How can we be sure it's not a trick? It sounds altogether too perfect to me — even the greatest castle has its termites, you know."

"Now Giraldus, I appreciate your concern —and yours too, Estivus — but who on earth would ever want to trick us like that? And besides, everyone else here believes in it, so why must you two be so stubborn?"

"Oh twaddle!" said Giraldus. "And the world has believed in a good many other ridiculous things that I'd want no part of either. Isn't that so, Estivus?"

"Absolutely, positively, indubitably and indeed it's so!" he replied, joining Giraldus in a quadrille as they began to sing:

We'll tell you the tale of poor simple Rupert,
Who believed everything he was told
And wasted away on a cold winter's day,
Trying hard to turn lead into gold.

When he was a lad, his Grandpappy had said
That boys are much better than girls,
And the stodgy old pest said that all's for the best
In this best of all possible worlds.

"Now listen, my boy, for the world is a stage,"
Quoth the bothersome man from his bed,
"And fools will rush in to get seats on a pin,
Where the angels dare not even tread."

"So now the time has come, my lad,
For one such as you to leave home,
But never return, for soon you will learn,
That all roads will lead you to roam."

"Always remember what your Grandpappy says,
And you'll need no one else's advice.
Just don't take wooden nickels, sour grapes or sweet pickles,
And lightning will never strike twice.

So Rupert packed up his traveling shoes,
Some soap and some old soda bread,
And he set out in mirth for the ends of the earth,
Which he'd heard was as flat as his head.

"Is no news the good news?" he asked with a grin
To the first girl he met on the dunes.
She replied with a kiss, "Ignorance is bliss,"
And then sold him a bridge to the moon.

(Now here's where the tale takes a turn for the worse,
So now you must listen and learn,
For a bird in the hand's like a rope made of sand
When you've taken the tail of a tern.)

He then met a man with a bowl in each hand,
One of vegetables, the other of ham.
When asked which he'd eat, he said, "I never touch meat,
So I think, therefore, a yam."

Rupert followed this sage to a fork in the road
At the foot of the mountain of truth,
At which time they parted and Rupert got started
On his search for the fountain of youth.

He looked high and low thirty years and a day,
To find where the magic stuff flowed,
Yet all that he found was a hole in the ground
And a bad case of warts from a toad.

"The sky must be falling," said Rupert aloud,
"Or at least I've been told I must fear it.
But when it falls to the ground will it make any sound,
If no one's around who can hear it?"

So he settled right down to that hole in the ground,
Where he stayed 'til his end as we've said,
Feeding on bones and the moss that had grown
On the rolling stones inside his head.

The moral herein is to think for yourself,
And don't believe all that you hear.
Never judge at one look what's inside of a book,
Unless the cover is perfectly clear.

With two pirouettes and two gracious bows, the song came to an end.

"Well, Master Nick, have we convinced you to stay?" asked Giraldus, tucking his hair back beneath his cap.

"No," I replied, "but you were most entertaining all the same."

"I suspected as much," he said with a shrug. "But then, leave it to you to find out how deep the water is by sinking in it. At least take this with you if you must go."

In his outstretched hand, he held what appeared to be a tiny brass ear trumpet.

"What is this for?" I asked, examining the little trinket.

"For clear vision," he replied. "Things are often not as they seem."

Having long since learned not to question the cryptic Giraldus, I simply thanked him for his gift and put it in my pocket. Then, with a snap of the reins and a shout to the reindeer, I was on my way to what promised to be a splendid expedition. Of course, had I known what was really in store, I might not have been so hasty.

Since no children made their homes in the barren northern land, our journey took us through long miles of unfamiliar territories that were not pictured anywhere on our maps. But at last, by nightfall, we reached the very end of the northernmost reaches, where the trees gave way to immense walls of glacial ice. There, carved in neat, simple letters, stood a small wooden sign that read:

"Well, that isn't very helpful," I thought as I hitched the reindeer to a nearby rock. "Seeing as how I have no idea where 'here' is, it might just as well tell me that I'm not somewhere else."

Suddenly, from out of thin air, there appeared an elaborate tasseled cord with the message:

PLEASE RING FOR THE ELEVATOR

And so I did. Without warning, the ground beneath my feet gave way and I was sent tumbling head over heels before coming to rest with a bump.

Looking up, I saw another sign that read simply:

GROUND FLOOR

As my eyes grew accustomed to the faint light, I saw that I was in the midst of the most magnificent garden that ever there was.

The air was warm and delicately perfumed, and a closer look revealed that the flowers growing in each direction were thick with leaves of polished jade. Blossoms of turquoise, diamond and amethyst bloomed from every stem, each one bearing a different precious stone. From the marvelous rows of onyx trees grew sparkling fruits of silver and gold, and delicate spices that scented the air. In a corner of the garden, peacocks nestled in a grove of amber lilies, and behind them flowed a fountain of rose water. All around me, the trees were filled with plumed birds that changed their colors as they flew among the boughs. Never in all the world had I seen such beauty, and never had I heard anything quite like the voice that suddenly spoke from everywhere and nowhere at once:

What is your pleasure, Nicholas?

"Who said that?" I asked, startled.

I *did*, replied the voice, as sweet as honey. *But come, come; this is no time for such trivialities. You have traveled far to find something here, have you not?*

"Why, yes... yes, I have. But how do you know about me?" I asked, searching for the source of the voice. "And where is here, exactly?"

You are in the garden of wishing trees, Nicholas, and here we know all things. Now go ahead and make a wish, for it shall be yours. Everything is yours for the asking.

"I have heard that here is where I may find a most marvelous clay. That is all I ask for."

Why, of course, said the voice, tinkling like chimes. *But there will be plenty of time for that later — surely there must be something else that you want. Everyone always wants something, you see. What a terribly lonely place this would be if they didn't.... Now why don't you have a look around, Nicholas? The jewels are ripe for the picking, and you can fill up your pockets if you wish — you could be richer than all the kings of the world.*

"Thank you all the same," I replied, a bit uneasy with the course of this conversation. "I'm really quite satisfied with what I

already have. All I
ask is that you please show me
to the clay and I'll be going."

Oh come now, said the voice with an
unsettling laugh. *What about the fair Sara,
your beloved wife? Would she not like some
pretty things to make her happy? Why, she
could have comforts to last a lifetime.*

I began to protest again, but it was too late. The voice had already woven its spell. Images of fabulous wealth danced through my mind, and I thought of Sara lounging in a carpeted carriage, clothed in the finest silks and jewels. I imagined the two of us at a table laden with the rarest delicacies, while the elves served us from silver bowls....

From the deep fog of my reverie, I heard the voice again, goading me on:

And why stop with mere wealth, Toy maker? If creation is what you seek, then what need have you for common clay when I could grant you the power to move the sun and stars?

I became dizzy with visions of myself standing alone in the universe, rolling the planets like marbles, the moon in my palm and the stars in my hair. It all could be mine. But then, dazed though I was, I suddenly had the creeping sensation that something sinister was afoot. Why on earth was this mysterious voice so anxious for me to accept its fantastical gifts? And why did there seem to be a growing note of impatience in its tone?

It was then that I remembered Giraldus' ear trumpet. I wasn't quite sure how it would help me here, but if the Masterman said it would bring clear vision, then it was bound to be good for something. I fished the little brass trumpet out of my pocket and held it up to my eye. Nothing happened. I tried looking through the other eye, but still nothing happened. Well, it certainly wasn't helping my vision, but ear trumpets are for ears, I thought, and maybe this one was no exception. I held it to my ear and listened closely.

Then a remarkable thing happened: in the boughs above my head, a bird sang out in a burst of bright lemon yellow. From the distance, another bird answered in melancholy droplets of violet and blue. Wherever I turned, I could actually see each and every sound. Even the rustling leaves and the tiny breaths of insects were sights to behold, and my very own heart beat a vibrantly colored rhythm in the air. And then there was the voice; the voice that once had sounded so musical and sweet could now be plainly seen as the thick, dark, ghastly green smoke it truly was.

With the trumpet at my ear and my eyes open wide, I followed the trail of smoke down the twisting crystal paths until I came upon the tiny green flowers of a mugwort plant; the only weed to be found in the entire garden. I gave the weed a pull, a tug, and then a twist, and yanked it right out of the ground by its long, spindly roots. It was, as I suspected, not your garden variety weed. From the moment I plucked it free, everything all around me underwent an astonishing change. All at once, the beauty of the garden vanished; the jeweled fruits withered, and the trees all shed their jade leaves until only fierce pillars of cold iron and ice remained in their wake. Where the flowers had been, now bluebottle flies swarmed around the dangerous points of the thorns that jutted out from the ground. Instead of sweet spice perfume, a foul-smelling wind blew a deathly chill to my bones.

So startled was I by the sudden transformations that it took me some moments to realize that the weed I held in my hand was no longer a weed at all. In fact, while my eyes were on the garden, the plant had sprouted arms and legs in place of its leaves, and where the green flowers had bloomed, there was now a most gruesome face, surrounded all over by white curls of mad milkweed hair. Before I could do a thing, the strange little creature wriggled from my grasp and, stomping about on the ground, began to rant and rave like a crow swallowing gravel.

"Now you've done it!" it screamed, tearing at its hair. "Now you really have done it! After all my hard work, you had to go and do a thing like that! You think you're clever, don't you? Well, I'll see to it that you will regret this day, oh yes I will! Now out of my sight — begone with you!"

And with a wave of his hand, I found myself back above the ground, right beside the puzzled reindeer.

Well, I hardly need to tell you that we raced straight home like bears from a bee's nest, not casting a single glance behind us. Back at the workshop, in the comforting company of Sara and the others, I told as best I could of the strange enchanted garden and the mysterious man of the weeds. With his face all twisted up in a frown, Ciraldus asked me knowingly:

"Tell me but one thing, Master Nick, was the color of the little man's skin as blue as a berry?"

"Yes, it was," I answered. "Have you seen him before?"

"Oh, dear sir, it is just as I feared. The rascal you met was a weed indeed, and none other than that dastardly elf Hoarfrost was he! I can't imagine how he escaped, but thank goodness you found the ear trumpet in time to see what was really afoot!"

"Or at hand!" chimed in Jarvis with a grin.

"Or ahead!" offered Estivus, prompting ripples of laughter and a chorus of responses.

"...that's right! You really got a leg up on him by the skin of your teeth!"

"...now let's not split hairs, and get to the heart of the matter!" "...should we take up arms and stick our necks out?" "Enough!" cried Giraldus, quite seriously. "Now is no time for terrible puns. We haven't heard the last from that fiend yet, you mark my words. I know that there is more trouble still to come...

I can feel it in my bones!"

CHAPTER TWELVE
The Elliptical Ball

*I*ndeed there was more trouble to come, but its arrival was so innocent and quiet, like the roosting of a dove, no one among us really thought to call it trouble at first. It was an ordinary December morning, and things were still running as smoothly as ever when I left the workshop to gather timber and holly in the forest. Although I would not realize it until much later, in the time that I was gone the sinister seeds of forgetfulness had dropped down upon the elves and were sprouting into an oddity in three dimensions.

No one knew who had made it, nor exactly what had gone wrong, but there it was all the same: a scarlet-swirled elliptical ball that would not roll, could not bounce, and looked just like a candy-colored goose egg.

For an entire day in my absence, the workshop was a frenzy of activity as each elf tried unsuccessfully to fashion a proper bouncing ball out of this mysterious ellipse. They pulled it and they stretched it, twisted it and turned it, but try as they might, none of them could seem to remember how to make any sort of ball at all. Even Autumna the Ancient, who was said to have invented the sphere, could only get as far as a semicircle before she had to give up.

When at last I returned, the workshop was littered with rhombuses and rectangles, trapezoids and triangles and objects of every imaginable shape except round. To make matters worse, their stubborn elfish pride would not let them admit to any mistakes, so, simply assuming they were inventing new toys, I left them to their own devices. Looking back on it now, I should have suspected that something was amiss when Giraldus asked just what I did for a living, but being so used to his impish ways, I paid him no mind.

Soon enough, though, it became all too clear that a full-blown disaster was undoubtedly upon us. On the following morning, I was awakened from my dreams by what seemed to be the sound of the sky falling on our heads. Sara and I raced to the workshop, where we found the poor elves in a chaos of their own making.

"Whatever shall we do? Whatever shall we do?" they cried, stumbling this way and that amid piles of discarded toys and broken tools. In the far corner, I spotted a haggard Giraldus, his left shoe atop his head, trying to paint a jack-in-the-box with a hammer. Fearing the worst, I rushed to his side and urged him to tell me what had happened, but he simply replied: "I beg your pardon, but just who might you be, good sir?"

Clearly, I was on my own in the middle of a disaster in the works. Not even a single elf could recall how anything was done; which tools to use for what, which colors to paint the toys, nor how to make toys in the first place. And as if it were not bad enough already, the elves had actually begun to forget their own names. As the workbenches overflowed with blue fire trucks on square wheels and stuffed bears with seven legs, I set about righting all the wrongs and putting the workshop back in order.

Sara, meanwhile, had the notion to paint footprint trails on the ground so that the elves could move about without getting lost. She even covered them from head to toe with labels to help them tell their upsides from their downsides. Together, she and I worked as we had in the old days, sewing and tinkering without pause as Christmas Eve drew near. Even so, the great memory crisis that had beset the elves continued to make them as helpless as leaves in a windstorm.

Most peculiar of all, though, was the fact that Sara and I alone had managed to remain sound of mind, and I puzzled over this mystery for many a day until finally I stumbled upon the obvious: it had to be the wild sparrowgrass juice that only elves are known to drink. Sure enough, a quick test proved without a doubt that some fiend had been tampering with the sparrowgrass supply, for the forget-me-nots had been drained out of the brew. While I emptied out the culprit cask, Sara began to tell the elves sad stories until they had cried out the very last drops of that dastardly drink in a river of lost memories.

One might have thought that with the elves back to normal, the trouble would have been no more, but, alas, sometimes when bad things start to happen there is just no getting away from them until they decide to leave you be. So it was that, only moments after the last elf had dried away his tears, I made the terrible discovery that the reindeer had disappeared.

I raised the alarm and scattered the elves to all corners of the forest in a desperate search. We looked high and low from the nests of the eagles to the doorsteps of badgers, but neither hide nor hair nor hoof was to be seen. With Christmas Eve falling on the very next night, there was no time to lose. At the stroke of midnight, I called an emergency meeting to order, gathering all of our forces in the workshop for a brainstorming session.

"It's Hoarfrost who's done it!" cried Estivus, tearing at his hair. "Only he would dare to perpetrate such a pernicious performance! The fiend has returned to wreak his revenge!"

On into morning we fretted and fumed, but found ourselves stumped at every turn. How could we possibly hope to make the Christmas journey without the help of the reindeer? Eventually, as the dark sky paled with the daylight, Giraldus suggested the unthinkable:

"Oh, dear Master Nick, I fear to speak, but speak I will this truth: It is not upon you that the wicked Hoarfrost seeks to work his sorcery — it is I and my company that he despises. Perhaps if we were to surrender ourselves, then he might return the reindeer, and Christmas along with them."

"No, Giraldus," I replied. "A hundred times no, I will hear of no such thing. We are in this together, as we have been all along, and not even Hoarfrost will prevent us from staying that way — that is a promise. Now then, no more foolishness, we have business to attend to."

Just then, a loud clap came resounding from the other end of the table. It was Hibernius, madly grabbing handfuls of empty air.

"Hibernius, you loon," said Lapidus. "Have you finally gone mad?"

"Stark raving, if you must know!" retorted Hibernius, slapping his forehead. "It's all these pesky deerflies in here. They're driving me to distraction!"

"A short trip indeed," snapped Estivus. "If only you would wear your spectacles like you're supposed to, you would see that it's the dead of winter and long past the season for deerflies!"

"Stop! Everyone stand still!" I shouted, for at that moment I knew what had happened. I snatched up a magnifying glass and inspected one of the flies — and what do you suppose I saw but a little deerfly, sporting a tiny set of antlers and Prancer's telltale mark of the morning star.

With shouts of joy and sighs of relief, we scurried about to collect the errant deerflies, finding two in the sugar bowl, one on the ceiling, and three in my beard. In a stroke of good luck, Estivus found the last one dangling in a cobweb, just in time to save him from the clutches of a hungry spider.

Now, the only problem was what to do with eight deerflies on Christmas Eve. Some of the elves suggested shrinking both me and the sleigh down to deerfly size, while others proposed that we feed the flies until they got big enough to pull all the toys. Thankfully, the level headed Giraldus reminded us that Hoarfrost's magic could never truly change anything, it could only mix up what something already was. Thus, using his elfin logic, he reasoned that we simply had to find an antidote that would increase the flies' "deerness." With a flash of light and two wisps of smoke, the

Superior Elect Chemist, Emeritus, mixed up a potion of deer ferns, deer grass, deer's tongue herbs, and the tears of eight deer mice. Eyedropper in hand, he gently bathed the deerflies in the potion, restoring each one to his natural deerish dimensions.

Now at last, everything was back in order, and we were ready to embark on another carefree Christmas voyage... or so it seemed.

CHAPTER THIRTEEN
Hoarfrost

The evening that followed was like waking from one fevered dream right into another, each worse than the one before it.

From almost the instant I left the ground, the hobgoblins I had heard of in legend appeared in all of their swarming fury. Like moths to a candle, they hovered about the sleigh, screeching in my ears and plucking the hairs of my beard with their spindly fingers. They rang all the church bells to waken the towns, and they painted the sun on the sky so the roosters would crow for dawn. They stole stockings from some homes, while from others they snatched the Christmas trees and decorations. Those nasty creatures even went so far as to rip a hole in my toybag, nearly scattering all the presents into the cold Caspian Sea. Wherever I went, the hobgoblins overwhelmed me with their beady eyes and prying hands. There were goblins, goblins everywhere and not a stop to think!

Luckily, word of my peril must have been carried by the nightbirds, for it was not long before Giraldus, Estivus, and the entire elf cavalry arrived to do battle. Under the wintry moonlight they rode, atop hobby horses and wooden wagons drawn by teams of toy tigers. Behind them came a thousand tin soldiers with slingshots in hand, pelting our fiendish foes with snowballs and gobs of sticky treesap.

All through the night, my troops out-tricked those tricksters at their own game, trouncing the hobgoblins at every corner of the globe. They chased them from the rooftops, the rainspouts and the chimneys; they swept them away from the mountains, from the valleys and the fields. For each and every hobgoblin that lay in hiding, twice as many elves appeared to pluck it out like a rotten tooth.

At long last, when the night's voyage had ended, I returned home; cold, weary, and unaware that I was about to face the worst challenge of all — the wicked Hoarfrost himself.

In the bleak pale of early dawn, he appeared as he had once before, with skin the color of ice and eyes as fierce and depthless as cold metal. Beneath his untamed mane of hair, he glowered so that his pointed nose met with the tip of his chin. I stood before him, rooted fast to my path with fear and the icy chill of his presence.

118

"Well, well, Toymaker," he snarled, his breath stinging my cheeks. "Truly, you are a greater fool than ever I took you for. Do you not have enough sense to see that your efforts are useless? Now stand aside, for I shall have my vengeance on your miserable elves, and I will include you, too, if you try to stop me!"

"No, Hoarfrost!" I cried, mustering all of my courage. "I have no quarrel with you, but I will not allow you to bring harm to the elves. They are my family, and we watch over each other just as we watch over the children of the world. Even though you wish ill upon the elves, would you deny the children their happiness?"

"Happiness?" the ornery elf shrieked. "Bah! There is no such thing as happiness, Toymaker! Have you not spent enough time among the humans to know that they are nothing but a stingy, mean, and hateful breed? Your happiness is but a fool's illusion, old man. Don't you know what happens to your precious gifts?"

Hoarfrost's lips peeled back into a chilling grin, and he cast upon the ground a handful of cogs and wheels and springs. I watched aghast as they squirmed like blind worms in the snow until, meeting with one another, they formed themselves into mechanical figures with missing pieces and broken limbs. From their faceless heads, tiny voices came crying:

We are the shattered ones,
We are the abandoned ones.
When our use was no more,
All battered and sore,
We were left without home,
We are all alone.

Then, quivering, they collapsed into a heap on the ground and turned to rust.

"This is what happens to your beloved trinkets, Toymaker," Hoarfrost continued. "When the children have grown tired of their Christmas spoils, your toys are nothing but useless scrap and misery. And what do you think happens to the children when age has taken their youth? Think you that they will remember your wasted kindness? Then you know nothing of the human soul. Look you here, and I will show you things as they are, life as it is lived!"

Now I must admit that, though I have stood at the peaks of the Himalayas, where the earth drops off into mist, and though I have felt the chills of the Arctic wind's blast, neither could ever compare to the cold fear that held me fast as Hoarfrost wove his spell.

In the air above where the sorcerer stood, there appeared a spectral band of human figures, rapt in a dance of sheer malice and fury. I could only gaze in horror, growing colder with each passing second while the apparitions tore at each other's clothing with their bony fingers. With the faces of wild beasts, they turned toward me, snarling and gnashing their teeth as they circled about my head. The more they danced, the weaker I became, and my bones rattled beneath my skin as the specters began to chant:

Child who comes and child who goes,
  This is the way of all human souls.

Child who comes and child who goes,
  This is the way of all human souls.

  This is the way, this is the way,
  This is the way of all human souls…

Their bellies grew fat as they feasted on my fear until, opening their mouths wide in wicked laughter, they swallowed themselves up and were gone.

"There — do you see, Toymaker? This is all they are, your favored children, for all must march the way of their souls. But you, with your lies of goodness and caring, you have no place among them. When they are old and sour as grapes withered on the vine, they curse your name for cluttering them up with useless illusions."

I wanted desperately to cry out, to tell Hoarfrost that it was not so, but my voice remained frozen in my throat. I could hardly breathe another breath, and my body was slowly becoming encased in a prison of ice.

Then suddenly, just as I thought I could bear no more, a curious notion crossed my mind: for all of Hoarfrost's black-hearted rantings, he really seemed just like a spoiled child throwing a tantrum because he has been left out of the game.

Slowly, silently, I reached into the very bottom of my toybag and found that there was one last toy still waiting to be given. It was a little doll, no bigger than my hand, but it bore a most striking resemblance to the mad sorcerer himself. Not knowing what would happen next, I did what I do best. I gave him the gift.

To my surprise, the raving Hoarfrost was struck dumb in the midst of his tirade. Flabbergasted, he scowled at the little doll in his hand.

"Mama," said the doll.

Hoarfrost flew into a rage and waved the doll about wildly, as if to smash it on the ground.

"Mama," said the doll.

Oh, how he fumed and fretted now, stomping up and down so that the earth shook beneath my feet. Yet for each curse he would utter, "Mama" was all the doll would say.

All of a sudden, I found the whole spectacle so absurd that I could not contain my laughter, which drove the sour old elf into a purple-faced fit. At last, trembling mad, Hoarfrost let out one last piercing shriek and consumed himself in a cloud of icy-blue smoke. And, of course, he took the doll with him.

That night, when all was quiet once again, Giraldus and I shared a cup of victory cocoa and discussed the evening's events.

"Now tell me truly, Giraldus," I said with a wink, "just how did you manage to get that doll of Hoarfrost into my bag? I was absolutely sure that it was empty."

"I'm sure that I don't know what you mean, Master Nick," he replied without so much as a hint of mischief. "I will tell you now as I will tell you always that I had nothing to do with it — and that goes for the rest of the elves, too, for there was not a toy in that bag that I did not personally inspect."

"Well, if you didn't make it and I didn't make it, then exactly who did?" I asked.

"Let me tell you what I think, Master Nick — I think that yours is the power to make wishes come true, and I'll bet you my beard that old Hoarfrost had been wishing for that toy all along. You mark my words — next year he'll be wanting another. You see if it isn't so!"

And it just so happened that the very next Christmas, on a tumbledown chimney, amidst the rubble of an old | burned-down house, I came upon a sight that I never thought I would see. Some of the stockings that had been stolen the year before had been crudely stitched together into the largest ragtag stocking I had ever laid eyes on.

Knowing in an instant that it could only have been the work of Hoarfrost, I placed a single toy at the bottom of the greedy elf's stocking and went on my way. From that day on, I have never had much more trouble from Hoarfrost — except for an occasionally bitter chill on the wind — and that year marked the beginning of a tradition that we have continued ever since. And every Christmas that monstrous stocking reminds me of how two old foes made peace after all.

CHAPTER FOURTEEN
Forevermore

*M*any years had passed, and as time turned with the turning world, the battle with Hoarfrost had long since taken its place among my distant memories. But then, as I entered my one hundred and tenth year — which is a good long life by any measure — I came to know a fear far greater than any other: the fear that my wondrous journey might at last be near its end.

Though I still felt the fires of youth in my belly, it was true that my bones could no longer carry the weight they had in the past. As the stiffness of my hand and the wandering of my eyes could attest, the Yuletide voyages had finally taken their toll, leaving me all too aware that even I would not be able to carry on the gift-giving forever.

In the quiet of one midwinter's afternoon, Sara and I left the workshop to walk through the snow-dusted forest and talk of the uncertain days that lay ahead. Another Christmas had just come and gone, and thoughts of the joy I had been able to share with the children of the world helped to brighten the darkening day. My life had so long been inseparable from the lives of these children; I knew the names of each and every one of them, their hopes and their dreams and their sadnesses too. I had watched them grow with as much pride as though they had been my own. Now what would happen to them, to their belief in magic and miracles, when I could no longer make my visits? What would happen to the dream if its dreamer were no more?

Such melancholy thoughts burdened my mind, and I spoke them aloud to Sara until tears welled up in my eyes and fell silently to the ground. And then a mysterious thing, a thing most magical and fantastic, began to happen.

From the very spot where my teardrops had struck the frozen earth, the new green shoots of a poppy flower sprung forth and burst into a magnificent bloom. Within moments, the wintry forest came alive with the sight of flowers pushing up through the crust of the snow. On the breath of a gentle breeze, I heard again the music of delicate woodsprites, dancing and chiming to the notes of Elder's pipes. I held Sara's hands tightly in mine, and trembling with

delight, we watched the sprites flicker through the transformed forest, lighting the way for a parade of jubilant elves. Above it all, there hovered the green-robed Elder, astride the back of a tremendous iridescent butterfly. The chattering crowd fell silent as Elder descended, greeting me for the first time since our distant dreamtime meeting in the chasm.

"Long has it been, yes, friend Nicholas? But I can see in your eyes you have been thinking of time. Such thoughts must not bring you sadness, no, for time cannot take what is not its own."

He smiled a broad smile, and even the elves fell to a hush as he continued to speak.

"It came to pass, yes, in the days of Great Elfhame, that a certain clan of elves dwelt in harmony with the mortal humans. This, you see, is where the story will begin, and in the end, which has not yet happened, we will arrive here, at the middle, for the story is your own, Nicholas, indeed it is.

"Over the course of the centuries, in the riverbed of the past, the elfin and human peoples became as one. Unique in all the realms of the world, they were. Yet not many in number was the community of these special kinfolk, no, and so it happened that, in the age of explorers, when humans pushed the elves into the shadows of hidden places, this fragile breed all but disappeared. In time there came a day — a day of little light, it was — when the very last of their infants was born into the world. It was decided then, by the Council of Ancient Venerables, that this child would be the son of mortal parents. He would live out his life in the world of humans until, at the end of his allotted time, and only if he had proven himself good of heart, he would be granted the immortality of the elves. Thus would this child grow to learn the way of the mortals and be the one and everlasting link between the magic of the ancient earth and the peoples of the new human sphere.

"That child was you, yes, Nicholas, and the path you have taken is the tale nearly told...."

Only as the ageless elf spun the last threads of his story did I realize that evening had crept across the sky. Slowly, the poppies began to close one by one in the light of the full moon. Elder summoned me to step forth, and I saw that in his hand he held a basin made of lotus flowers, into which he had collected the water of my fallen tears. I approached and gazed into the shimmering basin. There, gazing back at me, was the reflection of myself as a young boy.

"Yes, good Nicholas," said Elder. "The waters speak the truth, that they do. Only now have you lived long enough to know the child that you shall always remain. That which dwells in the heart can never be lost to the spirit." This last part he spoke without words, only with his eyes.

On the surface of the water, there appeared the reflections of two brilliant stars, and Elder motioned for Sara to join me. At the old elf's word, we reached into the basin and plucked out the stars. Just as we did so, I could feel myself growing stronger as the weight of the long years lifted from atop my shoulders like a wish borne on dandelion down. Silently, the last poppy's petals closed, and Elder began to vanish from sight, remaining just long enough to speak his final words:

"In this end is to be your greatest beginning, Nicholas, for from this day forth, the world will know you as Santa Claus, The Keeper of Childhood Dreams. So has it always been, so shall it be forevermore."

The elves erupted in a glorious cheer that shook the snow from the treetops and began a revelry that has been remembered ever since as The Night The Hills Sang Out. Hand in hand, Sara and I turned to join the joyous elves, dancing as never before beneath a universe of infinite stars.

By the Inkwell

*I*t can never be known how this story will end, for in a life that lasts forever, there are no such things as endings. Throughout the many centuries that have passed since those long ago days of my youth, I have gone on to have some of my most fantastic adventures in the hidden corners of the world. Here, beside the inkwell, as the last drops of ink are drying on this very page, I could fill my pen once more and tell of the magical places that I have seen; of places where luminous birds bathe in the lake of green tea, or of shining cities in the trees where children grow from the branches like leaves. I could tell of the splendors of the Kingfisher's courts or the Blue Heron's ball where once I danced to the waltzes of the fiddler crabs. Or, if you wish, I could speak of the caverns beneath the sea and the tiny colored fishes who whisper of sunken ships and buried treasures.

But these are stories best saved for other times, for there are so many wondrous places in this world that I could never hope to squeeze them all in here. From these secret places, I have collected tales to fill a thousand volumes more, each one a single chapter in a story of which this book was really only the beginning. So perhaps on a cold Christmas Eve when the moon is brightly shining, you may hear me knocking softly at your window. Come along with me then on a sleigh ride to the stars, and I will tell the rest to you.